GUNS, GAMS, GHOSTS AND GANGSTERS

TURNER HAHN AND FRANK MORALES CASE FILES
BOOK 2

B.R. STATEHAM

1

THE LOVELY IRENE

So, in a nutshell, this is what went down. See if you can figure it out.

The body was found sitting upright on a toilet bowl, slumped over onto one of the metal walls of the toilet booth, very much dead. Apparently due to the blade of a very large knife sticking out of the man's chest. The guy was in his mid-thirties, an accountant at a large bank, unmarried, who was said by friends and relatives to be a very nice man without an enemy in the world.

Well, you know—there seemed to be something wrong with *that* picture.

Sitting on the tile floor to the right of the toilet bowl was a large leather briefcase: untouched and very heavy. On the small coat rack on the back of the toilet stall door was a heavy but expensive looking trench coat still partially wet from the downpour raging outside like a madman's nightmare. When the body was discovered an hour prior, the building's security officer swore there was a set of wet tracks leading into the men's room and straight to the stall the dead man now occupied. Just one set of tracks.

A quick scan of the building's security cameras clearly showed the deceased stepping out of the elevator and into the building's lobby. Three different cameras in the lobby showed the victim walking across the wide lobby floor, briefcase in one hand, a wet trench coat in the other, as he headed for the Men's Room. Then the victim walked into the restroom and never came out. No one else entered the restroom until about thirty minutes after the deceased, when the security officer, who was making his nightly rounds, walked into the restroom and found the dead man.

Now, here's the interesting twist. There was no blood. No suspects. No way for a killer to *enter* and/or *exit* the scene of the crime without being recorded on the cameras. Maybe this comes as a shock to you, bubba, but stick the blade of a long knife into a man's chest and there's blood everywhere. But not this time. Not one drop of blood anywhere. *Including* in the dead man.

When our little, gum-chewing forensics specialist Joe Weiser told us about no blood in the body and no blood to be found in the entire men's room, I had to grin, shove hands into my trousers' pockets, and turn to one side and stare at my partner. Frank Morales, for those who are uninformed, is a Neanderthal. Well, not *really* a Neanderthal. But the guy looks like what one would *think* a modern Neanderthal might look like. A jaw made of bone so thick he could chew reinforced concrete for a snack, no neck to speak of, with the brightest looking carrot-colored red hair that absolutely refused to be combed. His overall body shape was that of a cement block, albeit one that stood about six feet four. Big, tough, and strong. One's natural inclination is to think someone that good looking had to be as dumb as a bag of marbles. But, oh brother, would they ever be wrong.

He eyed me with his dark browns, made a sour looking face, and rumbled like a badly tuned Russian reactor.

"I hate shit like this. Hurts my head. I think I'll go to the car and eat some tacos. Call me if you need me."

He turned and began walking away. Not toward our car parked out by the curb in the driving rain but towards the inside of the office building. Grinning, I knew he was heading back to the security office to review the tapes again. I turned and walked back to the men's room for a second peek.

Now ask yourself this. How the hell does a guy step out of an elevator, walk across an empty lobby of a very large office building at two in the morning on a rainy Sunday, enter a men's room, and get a heavy looking butcher's knife rammed into the middle of his chest. By himself. No one is in the men's room waiting for him. No one *leaves* the men's room after the deed is done. Is this a murder? Or a fairly gruesome suicide? Glancing into the stall I had to hand it to the guy. If this was a suicide, the bastard was committed in ending it if he shoved the knife into his heart all by his lonesome.

But I didn't think it was suicide. People usually don't kill themselves like that. Especially a successful, happy-go-lucky guy like that.

I went over the men's room again diligently. Looking for something, anything, Frank and I could have missed the first time around. Forensics had come and gone, finding nothing out of the ordinary. I had this nagging little voice in the back of my head telling me we were overlooking something. Something small. Something obvious. But something important. But that was the problem. I hadn't a clue what it could be. Frustrated, I walked out of the men's room, strolled across the empty lobby with its polished, black tile floors, and came to a halt in front of the bank of elevators sitting in silence all in a row. Specifically, I stood in front of the one the dead man used just before he checked out. Permanently.

Pushing the 'up' button the black doors of the elevator opened with a vague hissing sound and I stepped in. The doors slid closed behind me and everything went silent. Forensics had been all over the elevator. There were about a million different prints lifted off the controls, the hand rail circling the interior of the car, and off the doors themselves. It would take weeks to sort through them all. Turning, I punched in '10' and felt the elevator car lurch into motion and begin its ascent. Why '10,' you ask? The tenth floor was where our dead guy worked. Big accounting office. Lots of number crunchers working there. Everybody gone, of course, over the weekend. So why was our man here in the building at two in the morning on a Sunday?

Dunno.

But I began walking the empty hallway of the tenth floor, curiously eyeing all the empty—and locked—offices. The hall lights were turned low. Shadows played across the walls. It was as quiet as a monk's cubby hole. Don't know what I was looking for. Didn't expect to find anything. Actually, I was kinda shuffling around like a lost deer, that nagging voice in the back of my head getting louder and louder. I couldn't figure out what it was that was bothering me. I combed the tenth floor, then descended to the ninth and did the same ambling shuffle, before dropping down to the eighth.

On the eighth, I found a couple of items that caught my eye.

The first thing was the shine on the highly polished tile floor. Even in the dim light of the empty floor the shine was instantly visible and just as impressive. This was the Markle

4

Building on Hesston and Seventh Street. Ten floors of solid black and chrome from sidewalk to roofline. Black glass everywhere with long columns of chrome steel in vertical slashes for contrast. A stunning architectural feast to the eyes. The interior floors were black tile, kept to a glistening polished sheen.

The moment I stepped out of the elevator I noticed the floor. Maintenance had just finished polishing the tile. It was plain as day. There wasn't a scuffle, or footprint, or even a particle of dust anywhere on the floor from the elevator doors out for maybe twenty or thirty feet. But past the first two set of offices was a door which led into the building's stairwell. That's where I observed curiosity number one. The unmistakable wobbly tracks of someone pushing a heavy four-wheeled cart over the floor and stopping in front of the stairwell door. You know the kind of cart I'm talking about. The kind where you load up boxes and crates and push it from one place to another. The kind used mostly in office buildings to cart around bags of mail and other things.

In the dim light, I noticed the tracks hugging close to the wall and disappearing off into the shadows. Curious, I followed the tracks, and that's when I saw it. The bright and colorful neon lights of a building from across the street flashing through the glass walls of the Markle Building, continuing on through the clear glass interior wall of a set of law offices and playing across the black tile of the floor in a long, narrow band of multi-colored light. And there it was. About the size of a new pencil eraser. A bump of congealed blood.

Kneeling, balancing myself on the balls of my feet in the darkness of the hall, I stared at the lump of blood for a second or two. And then I looked up and at the doorway from where the cart's tracks originated from. It was a set of double glass doors with large gold lettering splashed across the glass announcing who was inside.

Schumer & Schumer Investments.

And it hit me. That nagging voice. I knew what it was trying to tell me. The dead man's rain coat. The tapes showed our dead man stepping out of the elevator *holding* his damp raincoat draped over one arm. A *damp* raincoat. Not a soaked to the bone—"Yes, I have been swimming in a 'fracken monsoon,"—kind of wet coat. Just damp. As if he had already been in the building for a while before riding the elevator down to this death. Schumer & Schumer's assigned parking stalls were on the top floor of the parking garage next door. The investment firm also had its own private entrance, which connected their offices directly to the parking building.

Standing up, I stepped over the lump of blood and approached the glass doors of the investment firm. They were locked. I stepped back, frowning. I jumped slightly when the cellphone inside my sport coat suddenly went off.

"Yes?"

"Get down to the security office, flatfoot. I've got something to show you."

I stretched a half-grin across my lips. Frank calling me a flatfoot was funny. Especially if you ever saw his feet. Flatfoot is also a rub for uniformed police officers, which we both had been earlier in our careers.

"Got something to tell you as well, dear," I said, smiling wider, "but do me a favor. Find the building supe and tell him to come up to the eighth floor and unlock the offices of Schumer & Schumer. We need to look inside."

A couple of minutes later I stepped into the crowded clutter of a small office in the basement used by the building's security staff. One wall was filled with computer monitors. One wall was filled with shelves full of various video tapes, boxes of digital equipment, and training tapes. A third wall was lined with metal storage cabinets with the names of various security employees with sticky labels on them. There was a desk, an office chair, and more computer screens in the middle of the room. Frank was standing by the wall of computer screens with a remote clicker in one hand, studying a monitor closely.

"Whatta ya got?" I asked, closing the office door behind me.

"Whatta you got?" he grunted.

I told him about the eighth floor, the cart tracks, the blood sample, and my theory about our dead guy and his rain coat. He grunted and nodded his head.

"That explains why I haven't found a tape of our guy returning. I've got an image of him leaving Friday night around a quarter to seven. But haven't a clue as to when he came back to the office. But I did find something else. You'll want to see it."

He lifted the clicker in his hand, aimed it at one monitor, and clicked it. Instantly the images of the lobby from some earlier time began rapidly rewinding.

"Watch."

I watched.

Frank clicked the clicker in his hand again and the rewinding stopped. Images began flowing normally. An empty lobby in the early morning, and then traffic—lots of traffic. Men and women in work clothes and carpenters, plumbers, and electricians coming in and filling the lobby and going in and out of both the women's and the men's restrooms.

"The supe said both restrooms have been extensively remodeled. Workers came in around noon yesterday, put up 'Out of Service' signs everywhere, roped off the restrooms, and didn't leave until seven p.m. last night. Now watch. We're coming up to when they finished."

My eyes went back to the monitor. The images began to move. Everyone was cleaning up and preparing to leave. They did so in ones and twos, with everyone gone around 7:23 p.m. At 7:28 p.m. a worker, pushing a heavy looking four-wheeled cart in front of him, rolled into the frame and disappeared into the men's room. On the cart was a large cardboard box. Very large. Ten minutes later, the figure, still pushing the cart with the large box, rolled out of the men's room and disappeared off screen.

"Did you catch it? Both of'em?"

I threw a questioning glance at Frank and then looked back at the screen as he rewound the images again.

"I saw the guy moving the cart a hell of a lot easier. Like whatever he was rolling into the pisser seemed to be a lot lighter when he was leaving."

Frank, twitching the corner of his lips visibly, told me he was silently amusing himself on my near sightedness. So I stepped closer to the monitors and took a second look. The worker went into the men's room with box and heavy cart. He —maybe—was around five-foot eight. He was thin, and he wore a baseball cap pulled low over his face. There was no way to make an identification. But, eyes narrowing, I finally saw it. I turned and looked at the lip-twitching sonofabitch.

"A woman?"

Frank nodded and then lifted the clicker up and began fast forwarding through a number of other images.

"Security tapes get replaced every twelve hours. Noon and midnight. Watch this."

My eyes went back to the monitor. It was our dead man stepping out of the elevator and walking to his death. He walked into the rest room and, maybe twenty-five seconds later, the door to the restroom moved just a hair. It was hardly notice-able. Unless, of course, you were looking for it, which appar-ently, Frank had been.

He raised the clicker and froze the image on the monitor and looked at me. I looked at him, shrugged, and improvised.

"Only thing I got is our killer was dressed up as our victim,"

I said, "and that the real victim was dead long before she dressed up as him. She delivered him disguised as a plumber. He's stuffed in that box. She dumps the body, leaves, then dresses up as the victim and deliberately allows herself to be taped stepping out of the elevator and heading for the restroom. My, my, my, a clever little girl. She hoped to give us an impossible crime to solve, thus giving her time to make her escape."

The red headed giant grunted, nodded, and folded his massive arms across his chest.

"So how did she stop the camera?" my partner asked.

"With the same clicker you have in your hands. She cracked the door open just enough to aim it toward the security office. Apparently, it has a long enough range to turn off the recorder. She walked out of the restroom and dubs the tape with the images she wants recorded once she's in the clear."

"Good. We know how the murder was done. We have a vague idea of a possible suspect. We know who our real victim is. But we really know nothing. Where did the murder take place? What, if anything, did she steal? And why was our accountant murdered?"

I grinned savagely at the big guy. He frowned, turned toward me, and tilted his head to one side curiously. I'm told Frank has an IQ of about two gazillion. But he hates it when someone else comes up with something he missed. Like now.

"Spit it out, Sherlock. I'm all ears."

"Two things," I said, still grinning like a malicious elf. "One, did you talk to the security officer on duty tonight? I didn't. Did you?"

"No," Frank growled, shaking his head. "The uniforms did. They relayed to me the information he gave them."

"Not him, my overgrown little Watson. Her. *She* told the uniforms everything she knew and then left the building. Said she had to get to her apartment at a certain time so her baby sitter could go home."

"So our killer worked the building in the capacity of a hired security guard. Meaning she had keys to get herself into practically every office in the building. Hey, I like that. Smart. Now, tell me what else that little peanut brain of yours has cooked up. I'm dying to hear it."

"Schumer & Schumer. What are they known far?" I asked.

"High end investments. Specifically, stocks and bonds." Frank answered, a light bulb suddenly going off in his eyes. "Oh, okay. I see it. The chick comes in and steals a shitload of untraceable bonds. Old bearer's bonds from way back when. God only knows how much she took. Probably millions."

Confession time. I'm rich. No. Not bragging. Just telling the truth. I'm a rich homicide detective. A few years back a grandfather I didn't know was still alive walked into my life and handed me an inheritance. Millions of dollars in cash, stocks, bonds, and real estate. I've been trying to play it smart and invest it ever since. So yeah, I knew Schumer & Schumer quite well.

"We got a killer running around town lugging a sizeable amount of very valuable paper. She can't fly commercial and go through the security checks with all that paper on her. TSA would ask too many questions. The bonds have coupons which must be personally exchanged at a bank to get the money. They're stolen. We'll have every bank and investment firm in town alerted to be on the lookout for them by tomorrow night. She's killed someone to get the bonds, so she's not eager to stick around town any longer than she has to. What's her only option?"

"She has to bite the bullet and sell them off at a steep discount rate," Frank said, his lips twitching suddenly in laughter. "If she's lucky she might get a quarter on a dollar. But the fence has to be a big one. Someone who can handle that amount of money in a few hours. That means her options are equally limited."

"Not just limited," I said, smiling as well. "There's only one guy in town who can come up with that much cash on such a short notice. That's where we're going right now."

It was the first faint light of dawn when we blasted across town in my white '65 Shelby Mustang. Where we were going the traffic was light. So we drove fast. And the Shelby, being a Shelby, with that small block Ford V8 in it, just purred.

The house was a mansion. A mansion pushed back deep into foliage with a long driveway that curled around in front of the house and disappeared back in the direction we had just traveled from. There were no lights on in the house. Except for one, to one side, in a wing of the house we knew to be the library. Yes. Frank and I have been at the house before on official business. We knew the place quite well. The owner of the house was a fat guy by the name of Lewis Hayden. A procurer of anything stolen which promised a very high pay off. Like, for instance, stolen bearer's bonds.

We walked around to the library, guns drawn, and peered in through the windows. Sitting in a big chair about the size of something a Nero Wolfe would sit in, a maid was placing three glasses of freshly drawn beer onto a coffee table in front of Lewis. The fat man nodded and mouthed the words, "Thank you." The maid walked out and closed the double doors of the library behind her. There was no one else in the room. Only Lewis, and *three* glasses of beer.

It looked ominous.

Using the barrel of my weapon to tap on the double French doors, we watched the big man rise out of his comfy chair and waddle across the carpeted floor to open them.

"Ah! Detectives Hahn and Morales. What a lovely

surprise. I was told I would be visited soon by the city's finest. Come in, come in. I took the liberty of having refreshments at the ready in anticipation of your arrival."

We stepped into the library and followed the round frame of Lewis Hayden back to his behemoth of a chair. Ponderously, he lowered himself into it and reached for one of the large glasses of cold beer.

"Please, gentlemen. Partake. I know you, Sergeant Hahn, to be a devoted aficionado of the hops. This is a rare brew direct from Germany. Not sold here in the States. I'm sure you'll find it most delicious."

"Who told you we were coming?" Frank growled, eyeing the dark colored beer before forcing himself to turn his attention back to our host.

"A delightful young lady for whom I have a most profound admiration for."

"What's her name?" I asked, turning my head and eyeing the interior doors of the library. The same doors the maid had just exited through.

"Oh, a most delicious irony there, detective. Most delicious indeed."

"She came here and sold you some old bearer's bonds. Obtained through a theft, and I might add, she committed murder in the process."

"Really?" Hayden exploded, astonishment on his face. "I was not aware of any such crime, or set of crimes, my dear detective."

"If you have the bonds in this house, that makes you are an accessory to murder. You know that don't you?"

"I am completely at a loss for words, Detective Morales."

"We could search the house," I said.

"You would need a search warrant, my dear boy. I would

insist. And obtaining one at this time of night? I daresay it would be an arduous process."

"How long ago was she here?"

"Why Detective Turner, I think you just saw her leave moments ago. Good luck finding her now. She is a most resourceful person."

I started to say something. But the house rocked as a big hammy fist pounded on the front door insistently. Frank glanced at me and nodded, before walking out of the library and into the main hall. Moments later, the big red-headed Neanderthal re-entered the library, followed by two uniformed officers bracketing the small frame of a red headed young girl. In the hand of one of the officers was a zip drive, which he tossed to me.

"Found her trying to hail a taxi at this time of night a quarter mile away. We thought that strange. So we picked her up and brought her over here. Knew you and Frank were working a homicide. Thought maybe there was a connection there."

Officers Flannery and O'Connor. Sons of Irish immigrants who became cops. From father to son. Both the best of the best when it came to police work.

I caught the drive, eyed it for a moment or two, and then smiled.

"Betcha this is the password for a freshly created bank account in some off-shore bank. Money transferred from your account into this one. With this little lady being the main recipient. If I'm right, both of you are going to jail for a long, long time."

Lewis Hayden looked almost sick. But give him credit, he was a showman who could not pass up wowing a crowd.

"Detectives, may I introduce you to a most charming young lady who calls herself Irene Adler."

"You're kidding," Frank, my oversized Watson, said, turning to look at the young woman standing between the uniforms, before turning to look at me again. "Well, Sherlock. You did it again. Congratulations."

Indeed, Watson. Indeed.

2

A BARKING DOG

E arlier, there had been something about the kid that bothered me. Well, maybe it was more what the kid had *said* to me that bothered me. Just a kid really. Maybe fourteen, fifteen years old. A geeky little kid plagued with adolescent acne and a love for video games. Rail thin with big brown eyes and wire rim glasses. A dime a dozen. You find'em in every apartment building on this side of town. At least one.

But the one thing Frank and I knew from experience was a kid like this knew a hell of a lot more than what he usually revealed. Not because he was up to some nefarious shenanigans. But because they just usually kept quiet and stayed out of everyone's way. Because, frankly, he *was* a geeky teenager with a case of acne with a connoisseur's intimate knowledge of the city's many pizza parlors.

Who the hell wants to be made into a laughing stock by a toothy-looking geeky kid?

Sliding hands into the pockets of my slacks, I stared down at the body lying on the worn-out carpet of the small apartment. The dead man's name was Tobin. Cory Tobin. *Councilman* Cory Tobin. Fifty-six years old, married, with two grown kids currently enrolled in some high-priced university on the east coast. His wife was rumored to be worth well over a billion dollars. That's a *billion* dollars. With a 'B' in front of the 'illions,' baby.

You see the conundrum.

What the hell is a man like Councilman Cory Tobin doing in a two-room efficiency apartment on that side of town? At that hour in the morning? With the handle of some kind of Oriental knife jutting out of his chest at a ten-degree incline?

Feeling the building shake ever so lightly I turned on my heel and watched my partner walk out of the small bedroom and set his course straight for me and the stiff lying on the floor. Big is a word one could use to describe Frank, like in, "*Jesus Christ*! He's a *big* man!" And they would be right. A little over six foot four, topping the scales around the three hundred mark, with carrot colored red hair that never stayed combed, a thick mustache of the same color, and a coating of carrot-colored fuzz for a beard. He viewed the world with little dark pin pricks for eyes that never missed a thing. Imagine that nightmare, buddy, and you'll have the perfect image of Frank Morales. My partner.

But make no mistake, hombre. Say whatever you want about Frank's size and looks. But never make the mistake that he's just a big dumb cop. Others have. Lots of others have. And they're upstate in one prison or another locked away behind bars for decades to come. The old cliché about your mistakes coming back to haunt you? Very true; very, very true.

"Nothing in the bedroom," Frank growled in his usual congenial self, stepping across from me and looking down at the corpse. "Hasn't been slept in for days. Nothing in the bedroom or the bath to indicate the councilman has ever been here."

"The girl?"

Frank nodded and turned his head to look back at the bedroom.

"Like the neighbors said. Young. In her twenties. No photos or anything like that. But she has expensive taste in clothes and shoes. Lots and lots of shoes. And this."

He turned back to face me, lifting the open palm of his right hand up toward me in the process. A curved jeweled scabbard. Oriental in design. A scabbard that would be about the right size for the blade buried deep into the councilman's chest.

"Chinese?" I asked casually.

"Maybe," Frank said, nodding. "Or possibly Korean. Either way, very old. Like maybe in the time of Genghis or Kublai Khan old."

"What's this girl's name?"

"Sandra. Sandra Shostakovich."

"So," I grunted, looking down at the body again, "we have a city councilman dead in the apartment of a young college girl at three in the morning and she's missing. Wonder what the newspapers are going to say about that?"

"Oh they'll come up with something," my partner grunted, the corner of his lips dancing around mildly. "But like Faux News on television. You know. Fair and Honest."

I almost grinned as I looked up at Frank.

"What do you think about the kid across the hall. What he said make any sense to you?"

Just after our arrival on the crime scene, Frank and I began talking to the neighbors closest to Sandra Shostakovich's apartment. Had they seen anyone coming or going? Had they heard any shouting or loud noises? Did they hear or see anything unusual? That's when the geeky kid chirped in. He looked up at us from behind his bank of expensive computer screens, sipping on a Coke straight out of a bottle in the process, and said he'd heard a dog barking. He said he was in the middle of a game of *Halo* around one thirty in the morning and paused long enough to go to the bathroom. As he was getting up from his seat he heard a dog barking, which, he said, was strange since no one he knew in this building owned a dog. The dog barked three times. Three times and then yelped in pain. As if someone had kicked it.

Yes, he said, he had heard the dead man walk down the hall and knock on Sandra's door after getting off the elevator. He didn't think anything unusual about that. Sandra always had men friends dropping in at unusual hours of the night. Usually college guys. Jocks, actually. But occasionally older men as well. Well dressed. Driving big, expensive cars.

Sure.

Sandra was a good-looking chick. Kinda like a hippie throwback. He said she liked long, cotton dresses with the tie-dye look and bangles and beads. Sometimes she played old classic rock n' roll songs a bit too loud. But she was too skinny for his tastes. Too skinny and dark-haired. He liked big-boobed blonds. The bigger the boobs the better.

That made me grin. Any chance this kid was going to get a girlfriend like that was out of the question. But I liked the kid's optimism.

"The dog comment sounded odd," Frank said, screwing up his face into an ugly mask. "His parents were sound asleep, so there's no one around to corroborate his story."

"Do we know anything else about her? Where she worked? If she had a boyfriend? Anything like that?"

"Geeky Boy says he thinks she just graduated from the university last winter and works at the museum down on Third Street. Doing what, he has no idea."

The museum on Third Street was The Otto Meier

Museum of Design and Technology. A big whale of poured cement painted blindingly white, with jet black glass dotting its exterior like some kind of disease. It sat on the corner of Third and Crescent. The exterior of the place was all curves. Not a straight line to be found anywhere. The interior was exactly the same.

We had to wait until around nine in the morning to find anyone in the building who might have known our victim. It took a little while to cut through all the intermediary staff to find someone who actually knew Sandra Shostakovich. But we were persistent. And Frank is just downright scary. After frightening about half of the museum's staff, we were finally introduced to a man by the name of Dr. Albert Brecht; Professor of Oriental History at the local university and head of the Far Eastern section of the museum's exhibition gallery.

"What?! Sandra is, is *here*? Here in the city?"

The color in the elderly man's scholarly face drained to an almost pure white when we told him of Sandra's demise. Both of us had to grab the man's arms and keep him upright as it looked as if he were about to collapse in front of us. Sitting him gently down on a bench, we sat down on either side of him and waited for him to regain his composure.

"But this doesn't make sense. She can't be here. At least, not in her own apartment. That's impossible."

"Impossible? How?" Frank asked bluntly.

The good doctor of Oriental History was in his late sixties. A small man with bushy white hair who gave me a vague impression of Albert Einstein. Well dressed, the little man was exactly what anyone would imagine an elderly college professor to look like. Except now, at this very moment, the good doctor looked almost terrified.

"We've just come back from a three-month expedition to

Outer Manchuria. Just arrived back in the States yesterday, as a matter of fact. I was about to, about to sit down and call Sandra's parents and tell them about the accident. I was interrupted, in fact, when I was told to come down and meet the two of you."

"What accident?" I asked.

"Five weeks ago there was a horrible accident. We were out on the high plains of Manchuria, standing on the edge of a rocky escarpment, when the vehicle Sandra was driving, for some inexplicable reason, drove over a cliff and fell almost three hundred feet into a ravine. The old thing just fell to pieces as it tumbled down the cliff. Sandra didn't survive. We found her mangled body at the bottom of the ravine. Mangled beyond recognition. But it was her. It was Sandra. I *know* it was Sandra."

"She's dead," Frank repeated, lifting an eyebrow in surprise. "As in, she's no longer here."

"Yes," the good doctor replied, nodding his head, eyes welling up with tears. "What a lovely child. Very smart. Extremely intelligent. Such a wonderful spirit, especially so after all the hardships she had to endure."

"What hardships?" I asked.

"Very unlucky in her personal relationships, detective. Poor child. Apparently, her fiancé, a boy off of the university's football team, committed suicide just before we left for Manchuria. It devastated poor Sandra. I thought she was going to drop out of the expedition. But she rallied, and like the budding scientist she was, she dived into our work the moment we arrived in Manchuria."

"Her fiancé, what was his name?" I said, reaching for the small spiral notepad I carried with me in a coat pocket.

"Rasmussen, I think. Vinny Rasmussen," the white-haired anthropologist answered, smiling sadly. "Nice boy. He loved

Sandra so much. He was devoted to her. But not a brain in his head, I'm afraid. Strange, isn't it. Smart people falling in love with someone far below their intellectual equal. I never could understand that. Still can't."

Sadness and regret mixed together like some glandular cocktail and passed across the professor's face. But outright fear kept the man's complexion a grayish putty color.

The fear.

That caught my attention.

"When did this Rasmussen kid commit suicide?" Frank asked quietly.

"Uh, uh, about a week before we were to leave for Manchuria, I think. Yes, that was it. A week before we left."

"Professor, did Sandra know a man by the name of Cory Tobin?" I asked.

"The councilman? Oh, sure. We all did. The Tobin Heritage Foundation helped finance our trip, you know. Big donation. The councilman was quite excited about it. He and Sandra were quite close."

For a couple of seconds we sat in silence and then Frank reached inside his sport coat and pulled out a clear plastic evidence bag. Inside the bag was the jeweled scabbard he found in Sandra's apartment.

"Professor, ever seen this before?"

Professor Brecht almost fainted. We caught him as he started to pitch forward and held him upright until he gathered his wits about him again. The gray putty color of his complexion had been replaced. Now it was the same color as a corpse. A corpse about six days old.

"Where, where did you find this?" he whispered, his voice shaking.

"In the girl's apartment," Frank grunted, one massive hand gripping the professor's left arm firmly. "Recognize it?"

"Absolutely! Sandra discovered it in one of our digs on the day she died. She was so excited about the find she jumped in that old jalopy she was driving and raced over to my tent to tell me about it. But she went off the cliff and . . ."

His body turned to putty again in our collective grips and he would have hit the floor if we hadn't held him firmly between us. But he eventually recuperated and assured us he was all right. Frank and I stood up to leave, but a thought occurred to me and, turning, I asked one more question.

"Professor, do you know if Sandra had a dog in her apartment?"

"A dog?" the professor echoed, blinking large brown eyes underneath shaggy eyebrows nervously as he looked at us. "No, not here. Not in her apartment. But in Manchuria there was this mongrel of a pup that kept following Sandra all over the place. Ugliest thing you ever saw. Sandra was quite captivated by it."

Frank and I nodded, glanced at each other, then left the professor sitting on the bench. As we walked out of the museum and headed for our car neither of us said anything. Eventually, Frank broke the silence.

"A barking dog."

"An ugly mutt left in Manchuria," I agreed, nodding.

"Curious," Frank grunted, opening the passenger side door and throwing himself into the car.

"Ain't that the truth," I said, climbing into the car and firing up the big V8 in front of us.

Curiosity.

In the end, that's it. That's the key ingredient to solving most crimes. That, and a big streak of sheer luck. Take for instance, the curious death of Vinny Rasmussen. Vinny was as big as a garage door and as healthy as a free ranging African elephant. A football player with some talent. Enough talent to really interest the NFL. He was also madly in love with Sandra Shostakovich. Apparently, she reciprocated his affections. The whole football team and coaching staff knew the two were an item. Everyone described Vinny as a big loveable kid who was about to get married. In fact, everyone we talked to said Vinny was living on cloud nine. Had everything going his way.

But then, inexplicably, he's driving back to the dorms in his old truck and decides suddenly to take a hard-right and smash into the cement column of a highway overpass a block away from campus. Just like that. Gone from being a happy kid madly in love to being dead. Very dead.

Why?

Here's where the luck came in. Checking over the notes of the detectives who initially did the investigation, we decided to look at the kid's cellphone. Three minutes before smashing into the overpass, Vinny got a phone call from Sandra. The call came from the museum. Her workplace. A little more leg work and we made an interesting discovery. When Vinny got that odd call, Sandra was *not* at the museum. She was sitting in the office of Councilman Cory Tobin talking about the upcoming expedition to Manchuria.

Half a dozen of the councilman's staff gave a statement confirming it.

Our curiosities peeked, we put in a lot more legwork. We contacted a number of museum and archeological students who accompanied the professor to Manchuria. We asked questions about the professor. About his relationship with Sandra. About the bucket of bolts Sandra was driving at the dig site. Our questions generated some interesting answers.

It seems like, some thirty years earlier, our professor Albert Brecht had had a torrid affair with a college student while he was a full-time professor at some out of state university. Very torrid. At one point the girl brought up charges against him.

She accused him of stalking her. But the charges were dropped mysteriously, and the student was never heard from again. We also found out that the night before Sandra drove over the cliff and killed herself, the professor was seen walking quickly away from the vehicle she had parked behind her tent that night.

So. We had two 'accidents' involving automobiles. With each of the accidents somehow related to our professor. We figured it was time to go back to the museum and talk to him.

Weird.

It was dark when we arrived at the museum. Long past closing hours. But we knew the professor was there because the answering machine on his phone told us he was working late. We parked the car close to the street curb in front of the museum and began walking toward the glass entrance of the giant building. It was a sultry, humid night. No moon. Still. Not a whisper of wind. The day's heat was radiating out of the sheet of cement that was the sidewalk and plaza of the museum in waves as we walked toward the museum.

And twice, I stopped, turned, and looked intently behind me. I'm still convinced, even now weeks later, I heard the sound of a dog barking. A single dog, barking angrily. But sounding as if it was off in the distance.

A barking dog.

I'm not a believer in the supernatural. I don't believe in ghosts. But the second time I turned and peered over my shoulder, Frank stopped and looked over his shoulder as well.

"You hear something?" he asked, glancing back in the same direction I was looking.

"A dog. Barking," is all I said.

"Huh," Frank grunted noncommittally, turning again and walking to the museum entrance.

We flashed our badges at the night security officer who was waiting for us at the entrance. He told us Dr. Brecht said we might drop in. We would find him in his office. It was a long walk through an empty museum. A dark museum with the lights turned low and all the display cases looming out of the darkness eerily as we walked past. Yeah, I don't believe in ghosts. But that's not saying I've not been spooked. Tonight was one of those nights.

It all happened so quickly. I still don't know why I reacted the way I did. I just did. *Instinctively.*

Frank and I marched through the mostly deserted museum, with Frank arriving at the door leading into the professor's lab first. Right behind him, I saw Frank reach for the door knob to open the door and heard a dog *barking* again. This time, the dog was barking louder than the previous two times and barking angrily and urgently. I reacted. Just as Frank's big hand clasped onto the door knob, I lowered a shoulder and tackled him. Hit him hard just above the hip bone and drove him down and onto the ungiving cement floor like the old defensive linebacker I used to be in my college days.

The moment we hit the floor together the bomb inside the professor's office exploded. There was a bone-rattling crash of noise, a brilliant flash of fire, and suddenly the semi-darkness of the museum was screaming with all kinds of bells and whistles from fire alarms going off. Smoke, billowing and thick, filled the air, along with long, searing fingers of flames. Frank and I scrambled to our feet and somehow got out of the place just in time. By the time the first responding fire trucks arrived on scene it was too late. The whole building was engulfed in flames. It took half of the city's fire fighting units and six full hours to defeat the flames. Hours later they found the charred remains of Professor Albert Brecht in his laboratory.

The professor left a note for us, in case we survived. He knew his luck had run out the moment Frank and I first came to talk to him. He killed all three in a fit of jealous rage. Vinny and the councilman for being interested in the woman he loved. Sandra in a fit of anger for being rejected. As simple as that.

No. I still don't believe in ghosts or the supernatural. But maybe, *maybe,* I'm willing to be a little more open minded about it.

3

COINCIDENCE

He was a tall, raw boned, old Irish cop whom my partner and I had known for years. Tall and lanky, with a face slammed together with red flesh and unforgiving bone. He had blue eyes and a nose the size of a Goodyear blimp. He could be as hard as tempered steel or as soft as a brand new pair of kid gloves. It all depended on the situation. But the guy was a legend. As a uniformed beat cop for twenty years, Joe Flattery, and his partner Paul O'Connor, had worked on maybe a hundred or more homicide cases. The two had seen it all. Every kind of murder. From crazies going berserk to crazies going all Dr. Moriarty on their victims. But as the four of us stood in the small strip mall office, one glance at the faces of the two uniformed officers told the complete story. This was a case neither wanted to work on.

The two were the first ones on the scene. They had interviewed everyone. And with each different witness they spoke to, their temperaments soured. By the time Frank and I got there, they were ready to climb into their patrol car and drive off into the darkness after handing the mess to us.

Can't say I blamed them.

"Let me get this straight," Frank, my partner, said, sounding somewhat confused. "All of the witnesses say they saw the shooter run into the office, screaming and waving a gun around, and shoot the office manager in the face."

"Correct," Flattery's third generation Irish voice leaked out as he nodded his head firmly.

"They then said, in unison, the killer ran to the back of the office and into a room that has no windows nor a door leading out of it except the one he used, and wound up getting shot himself?"

"And you have the full picture, me bucko," the blue uniformed officer nodded, looking relieved that someone had understood him at last. "The situation concisely stated. With the attending conundrum implied."

The four of us stood in the middle of the small office. Frank and I, the detectives assigned to the case, had just arrived. Flattery and O'Connor, the two uniformed officers and first responders, had caught the call a half hour earlier. The office was a twenty-five by thirty-five-foot office space in the middle of a strip mall complex of eight similar designed offices in one long brick and glass building. Plate glass windows to our right looked out into a wide parking lot; a sea of asphalt littered with a few late model cars and pickup trucks. On the other side of the parking lot was a Wendy's burger joint and a standalone building currently occupied by a retail bedding company.

In the office were inexpensive looking office desks pushed up against the walls, three per wall, with one larger desk, the manager's desk, in the back of the room and next to an open door leading into a small storage area. Up front, near the entrance, was a small counter where the loan company's only secretary would stand greeting customers as they entered.

The back room, by the way, was nothing more than an oversized closet. All four walls were nothing but large cabinets big enough to store a few boxes and mostly office forms. There were no windows in the room and the only way in and out was the one door that led out into the main office space.

A standard set up for a loan company. The kind one finds in every city across the country. Nothing special. Nothing odd. But . . .

"Again, I have to ask," Frank began, a hand coming up for emphasis. "The guy runs into the office. Runs to the back of the place where the officer manager is sitting and shoots the guy dead with a .38 caliber revolver. He then panics, runs into the storage room where there are no other doors or windows leading into or out of the room, and *he* gets plugged in the left temple with a 9 mm from some unknown shooter."

"That's it kid," O'Connor decided to chime in as he stood behind and to the left of his partner. "That's what all the witnesses said."

"Right," Flattery nodded. "All four of'em. Narry a word different in the way they described it. And now we give this mess to you. 'Tis a Merry Christmas to be sure!"

Big grins suddenly lit up the faces of the Irishmen as they stepped back and waved their goodbyes before turning and heading for the loan office's entrance, leaving the two of us standing in the front of the office wishing both of us were somewhere else.

Frank Morales is my partner of fifteen years. He's as tall as me but about fifty pounds heavier. He looks like an offensive tackle for an NFL football team that some outlaw genetics lab brewed up especially for them. Big, thick arms. Hands the size of dump trucks. A cement rectangular head with unruly, carrot colored red hair adorning it. And no neck. One look at him and you'd naturally think, *just another big, dumb cop one brain cell short of a half deck of cards.*

But brother, would you be wrong. All kinds of wrong. The old saw is true. Looks *can* be deceiving.

And me? People say I look like a dead man. A dead actor. Thick black hair that constantly has a comma of hair hanging over an eyebrow. A wiry black mustache. A permanent, cocky little sneer on my lips. Back in his day, this actor was a matinee idol. A big deal in Hollywood. Nope. Not mentioning any names. The guy's dead and you have to be a movie buff to think of the name. Which is okay by me. I hate being compared to a dead man.

So there we were, Frank and I, staring at the back of the office and at the door of the dead end room where our killer got himself killed by an unknown killer, asking ourselves, how do four people see something impossible happen? Or, the better question, who the hell shot to death our killer?

"I kinda think we ought to ask some questions," my genetic freak of a partner said, shrugging his shoulders. "You know, make an effort in solving the case maybe?"

"That would be a novel approach," I conceded as I grinned and nodded. "I mean, you know. They tell us we *are* homicide detectives. And this obviously is a homicide scene."

"A double homicide, Turn. Two . . . two dead bodies. That makes it a . . . a double homicide," Frank answered.

"Say, nothing gets past you, buddy. Honed right in on the obvious didn't you? I stand corrected. A double homicide. So what do you want to do first? Interview the four witnesses again and ask some different questions? Or wait and see if forensics can identify the dead guy?"

"Both," Frank grunted. "We do both. Might as well make an effort in earning our paychecks here."

So we went to work. We took our time looking over the crime scene and interviewing the four women who were present at the time of the shootings. Cop work is like that. At least, cop work if you're wearing a detective's badge is like that. You ask questions. Pertinent questions directly related to the crime. Tangential questions that have an offshoot relationship somehow to the crime scene. You ask personal questions to each witness as a kind of background info establishing the relationship with the witnesses to the victims. Eventually you start asking off the wall kind of questions. Questions that don't make sense. Or, at least, at first don't seem to make sense.

You'd be surprised what pops up in that last set of questions. More times than not they turn out to have a direct link to the crime scene. Like the question I asked to one of the women. She had mousey brunette hair, and she usually worked the front counter greeting customers.

"It was about lunch time when the murders took place. Did your boss usually go out for lunch or did he pack his lunch and eat in the back room?"

"Most of the time he just ate in the back room," she shot back before suddenly glancing sideways like some cartoonish character and breaking out into an evil little grin. "But lately, Mr. Roberts and Margie have been sneaking off together to get a bit to eat at the Chinese place down the street. Strictly hush hush, you know. Not supposed to happen."

I glanced at the list of names I had written down in the little notebook I used to scribble investigative notes in. There was no Margie listed. That sudden discovery of a possible new player, I thought . . . you know . . . maybe *should* be noted.

"Who's Margie? And why is a lunch date not supposed to happen?"

"Oh, yeah. You haven't met her. She wasn't here today. Off sick. She's Margie Waters. Another one of the loan consultants. And . . . and the sneaking off and having lunch together isn't supposed to happen because . . . well . . . you know. Both Mr. Roberts and Margie are *married*. Married to two different

31

people. You know . . . kinda on the sly these two. But not really. We all knew. We had a bet going on about it between us girls."

"A bet? As in . . . ?"

"As in who'd get the divorce first," the little mouse grinned widely, nodding in pleasure. "Had ten bucks riding on Mr. Roberts. The little weasel face couldn't keep his mouth shut if he tried. Sooner or later he was going to spill the beans. And when he did, officer, that would have been it. That will be all she wrote for that marriage. Believe you me!"

Cackling little witch. But, glancing back at the back room thoughtfully, this piece of gossip cast a new light on the investigation. Now Frank and I had three possible murder suspects. One being the unlucky Mrs. Roberts. The other being the just crowned grieving widow, Margie Waters. And finally, the cuckold husband to Margie Waters.

The wife of the first victim we ruled out almost immediately. She happened to be much older than her husband. By at least twenty-five years. She was in her early sixties and confined to a wheelchair due to arthritis and about a half dozen other age related infirmaries.

We eliminated the husband to Margie Waters almost as fast. Howard Waters was a petroleum engineer. Apparently a very good petroleum engineer. His work took him all over the world. At the time of the murder, Howard was working underneath a blazing hot Saudi Arabian sun in the middle of god knows where with only the men of one drilling rig and a couple of camels around him for company. There was no conceivable way Howard was going to fly back to the States, bump off his victim, and then get back to the Arabian Peninsula in less than twenty-four hours.

That left Margie Waters on our list. But she too became a problem.

Mrs. Waters was a petite, gorgeous creature who, before

marrying her husband, had had a really interesting employment history behind her. She had been at one time an actress, a professional dancer, a gymnastic instructor, and a circus acrobat. Yet what really caught our eye was another one of her traits. She had a large appetite for men. Mostly young men with lots of money and unencumbered with silly things like morals and ethics when it came to chasing married women. It certainly didn't bother Margie. At the very time both victims were gunned down, Margie was in a fancy restaurant four blocks away sitting down for a very expensive lunch with a young man who happened to be the son of a rich banker. About a half dozen couples were in the restaurant and testified that she and this young man arrived two minutes before the first victim went down and didn't leave the restaurant until an hour after the second victim was dead.

"Okay, Sherlock. We have a problem," Frank grunted, filling up the passenger side bucket seat of the '67 Shelby GT 350 Mustang we were driving that day. "Dazzle me with your brilliance and tell me what's going to be our next move."

We were sitting in front of the restaurant with both of us eyeing the clientele coming and going from the chic establishment. As we sat in silence, the fingers of my right hand were playing a little ditty on the wood of the car's steering wheel as I mulled over the situation. Yeah. We had a problem. Apparently our prime suspect for both murders had an unassailable alibi to back her up. In the cramped, dark interior of the Shelby I decided to voice a few ideas and bounce them off Frank's thick head.

"Hmmm, what's the motive of the guy coming in and killing the Roberts character? We know Roberts was probably boinking her for some unfathomable reason. But what about the guy who killed him? What was his motive?"

Frank's head bobbed up and down slightly in the darkness.

And then he reached into his sport coat and pulled out his cell phone and hit a speed dial number. Frank's deep, rumbling voice growled a couple of times in the darkness. But most of the time he just listened. In the darkness, I could hear the squeaky little voice on the other end of the line speaking through the phone's tiny speaker. But I couldn't make out anything. So I just waited patiently.

"Morgue just identified our first victim. His name is Javier Colonna. Apparently, Javier has had intimate knowledge of various detention cells and holding tanks at a number of different police stations across the country. Usually extortion charges. A couple of assaults. The guy had a reputation for having had a hot temper. But this'll get your interests up. He used to work for a circus as a juggler. The same circus our Mrs. Waters used to perform with."

"Well now, that's just one cupcake too many for a coincidence. You know what they say about murder and coincidences."

"You can have murder. Or you can have a coincidence. But you can't have both. It's like polka dot socks and a custom made silk suit. The two combined are a distinctive sartorial incongruity."

I grinned in the darkness. I couldn't help myself.

"Incongruity? Sartorial? Big words there, fella. Been on a reading kick? With a dictionary again?"

"Ha . . . ha," my partner shot back dryly beside me. "I have a few words I could use to describe you and your cutting witticism right now. Want to hear'em?"

"I'll pass," I said, the grin still on my lips, as I reached forward and hit the ignition switch to the Ford, the small block V8 lit up the night with a powerful low growl. There's nothing more pleasing to hear than the growl of a Ford V8 at a little past eight o'clock at night. Or eight o'clock in the morning for that matter.

"Where we going?" Frank asked as he turned his big head toward me and watched me slap the gearshift down into second before pulling away from the curb.

"Let's go talk to Mrs. Waters."

So we drove through the night on brightly lit streets. Just the three of us. Me, the big dork that was Frank, and the Shelby we were in. How many times before had the three of us done that very same trip? A dozen times? A hundred times? How many times were we going to do it in the future?

Hell. It didn't matter. And I didn't care. That's what we did, the three of us, we hunted. We prowled in the night like the hunters we were, and we enjoyed it. Enjoyed it more than any one of us would care to admit.

As we pulled into the dark residential street where Mrs. Waters lived, Frank's phone broke the silence again. Slapping it to his ear, he listened, grunted, then snapped the phone shut and slid it back into his coat pocket.

"Javier Colonna's bank account has almost three hundred thousand dollars in it, which is odd. Apparently Javier's been unemployed for the last year. Ever since he left the circus."

Up ahead was the ranch style house belonging to Mrs. Waters. It was brand new, with a three car garage and, glancing into the back yard, a rather large swimming pool. As we started to pull up in front of the house, we both saw one garage door move, spilling out a flood of light across the driveway. Pulling up against the curb a couple of houses away, I quickly killed the Shelby's light and sat back in the seat. In silence, we watched a new Lexus pull out of the drive into the street. As the garage door began sliding closed, the Lexus, with its lone passenger behind the wheel, began rolling away slowly.

I waited until the car slipped around the block's far corner before hitting the lights again and following. Keeping my distance, we followed Mrs. Waters half way across town. She apparently was in no hurry. Twenty minutes of driving time brought us onto another residential street, but one with considerably more modest homes. We watched as the Lexus pulled into a narrow driveway in front of an old two-story house. The lights on the car snapped off and then the interior light lit up as Mrs. Waters got out of the car and closed the door behind her. She moved down the sidewalk to the front porch. Half way to the steps of the front porch, a small porch light came on and the door to the house opened quickly. The silhouette of a rail thin young woman, with long hair falling past her shoulders, was outlined in the open door. Even from some distance away, we could see the woman standing in the doorway was wearing nothing but a slinky white slip over her hard body.

As we watched, we saw Mrs. Waters go up the three steps leading up to the porch and then straight into the arms of the woman. They embraced passionately, their lips locked on each other, and then disappeared into the house.

As they disappeared, Frank reached for his cellphone again. He listened intently to the voice on the other end far more than he spoke. When the conversation finished, he snapped the phone shut again and grunted in the darkness.

"Well now. Isn't this special," he growled, lifting one thick eyebrow in mild surprise. "Guess who lives here, buddy. Just guess."

I thought for a moment as the V8 rumbled in the night with enough torque and horsepower to make the car physically vibrate. And then I grinned.

"Javier Colonna."

"Bingo," nodded my partner. "And guess what. Betcha can't guess this one. Betcha."

"Mrs. Colonna used to work in the same circus as her

husband and Mrs. Waters. In fact, I'd say she used to be an acrobat herself."

"Exactomondo," Frank growled, almost laughing. "Ain't this special. Another set of coincidences. Whatta ya say we go down there and make our acquaintances. Should be interesting."

We knocked on the door loudly and waited. When the door opened, it was Mrs. Colonna in her white slip standing in front of us. Frank and I lifted our identification up and I started to try and say something. We never said a word. Instead, Mrs. Colonna rolled eyes up into her head and fainted dead away. Just folded up like a piece of discarded toilet paper and rattled to the floor in one big heap of arms and legs.

As we stepped over the unconscious form of Mrs. Colonna, we found Mrs. Waters sitting on a divan in the living room. On the coffee table in front of her was a cup of steaming hot coffee. And a gun. A 9mm Smith & Wesson MP.

The beautiful woman had the look of a fox tracked by a pack of blood hounds with nowhere to go. She glanced at the gun and then at us and then at the unconscious form of the woman still lying in the doorway. A sly little smile played across her beautiful red lips.

"She did it, officers. She's the one who shot and killed her husband. I'll swear it in court. She's the murderer."

"She may have pulled the trigger, Mrs. Waters. But I got a feeling you're the one who thought all this up," I growled as I sat down on the divan beside her. "So let's start from the beginning."

"What proof do you have I was involved in any of the killings?" she shot back, that smile was still on her lips as she folded her arms in front of her and sat back in the divan.

"Try this for size," Frank piped up, almost a smile on his lips. "The dead man's bank accounts? Guess what. Mrs. Colonna's name is not on the account. But yours is. I'd say that'd be a good place to start in breaking your alibi wide open. Wouldn't you?"

The smile disappeared from her lips. Fear slipped into her dark blue eyes. Slowly her folded arms in front of her unfolded and dropped into her lap. She was caught. There was no wiggling out of this one.

When the story finally came out, it was a sordid affair of simple basic greed. The three of them were all working together. Their line of work was simple extortion and black-mail. Find rich married men. Seduce them and suck as much money out of them as possible. Then discard them and move to a different town. The lonely, and quite plain looking, manager of a loan company, Mr. Roberts, wasn't worth a dime. But his elderly wife was. By several million.

But the homely Mr. Roberts was different. He had a brain and he didn't mind using it. He had figured out the woman he was spooning was bilking thousands of dollars out of him. He threatened to go to the cops. All three of them panicked. Mrs. Waters hatched a plan to kill the homely man in broad daylight in the office. After the murder, Colonna was told to run into the back room and escape through the rear door where a car would be waiting for him. What he didn't know was that there was no back door and no car waiting. Instead, Mrs. Colonna entered the loan office the night before and hid herself in the steel girders of the building's roof hidden by the white tile floating ceiling.

When Colonna bumped off Mr. Roberts after he ran into the back room, she lifted a ceiling tile and plugged Colonna with the Glock. Then she slipped the white ceiling tile back in place and waited. She made her escape later that night after the cops had come and gone.

Both women knew that Mrs. Waters would become the

eventual suspect. But she had an iron clad alibi. All that had to be accomplished was getting rid of the gun which killed Colonna. A minor detail both women were about to go through with when Frank and I came knocking on the door.

Coincidences. There's nothing like coincidences to muck up a good plan.

Any cop will tell you that. Just ask.

4

GONE SHOOTING

We came walking out in the bright sunlight of the hot summer afternoon shoulder to shoulder, my gorilla lookalike partner and myself, with both of us reaching for our sunglasses at the same time. It was August. It was hot. And the damn sun was gawdawful bright.

Slipping behind the wheel of the white '83 Chevy Z-28 convertible, I kicked the 350cu. in. V8 into life and slid the gearshift up into first just as Frank hit the play button on the disc and dialed up AC/DC's *Gone Shootin'*. With the six speakers of the expensive stereo working just fine, and with the top down on the convertible, I'm sure we rolled out of the back parking lot of the South Side Precinct entertaining anyone in the building who had a window open.

Up front, the engine rumbled and growled like it was supposed to. The car darted through the light afternoon traffic like a mountain cat on the hunt, and with the two of us sitting in the bucket seats, big boned and beefy as we are, I'm sure we were a couple of odd ducks to just about everyone we passed by on the streets. And yeah, brother. Frank and I are big boned and beefy. We both are a smidgeon over six feet four in height. I weigh around 250ish of relatively solid muscle. Frank is a hundred pounds heavier. A hundred pounds heavier and not an ounce of fat on him. But then, Frank's a biological freak who had to have escaped from some government genetics lab years ago.

And yeah, just to let you know, I've asked. He's never denied it.

Me—I'm just Turner Hahn. Normal. Well, *mostly* normal. Big, sure. And I vaguely resemble a famous actor from back in the 30's and 40's. But I try not to think about that. Gives me a muscle twitch every time I think about it.

It was seven in the evening, and we were going out to investigate a report of gunshots being heard behind an apartment house over on Haven & Fitzsimmons streets. Frank and I are cops. Homicide detectives. Normally, a pair of uniformed officers would check the report out first. But everyone wearing a uniform was busy between traffic accidents and working a major fire five blocks away from the call in. So Frank and I decided to check it out. Besides, we'd been at our desks writing reports from recently closed case files since we got to work at three that afternoon. We were more than ready to get out of the old precinct house and out into to the real world.

What caught our interest about the call was the location. The apartment house on Haven & Fitzsimmons sat in front of a sprawling old cemetery. A cemetery that went as far back, historically speaking to the founding of the city itself. Rumor had it the cemetery's oldest section was sitting directly on top of an old Indian burial ground. And yes, Maynard—the place was as *haunted* as they came. People, on a weekly basis, *swore* they saw ghosts in the place at night. Most of the people swearing out such affidavits, by the way, were the apartment dwellers living in that very same building.

Neither Frank nor I believed in ghosts.

On the other hand, people *swore* they saw strange things at night in the old cemetery. Things that supposedly would chill the blood of a Latin saint or a New England preacher. Make believers out of the most diehard of atheists. So . . . why not, we thought. Why not go check it out and hope it would have something to do with the cemetery and maybe . . . just maybe . . . a couple of ghosts thrown in for good measure.

The drive across town was pleasurable. The music was good. The sun felt pleasant along with the breeze created with the top down. It didn't take long to pull up to a curb directly across the street from the apartment building. The building was a red brick three-floor thing. Neither old nor new, but well-kept from the appearances of it. The small parking lot to one side of the building was mostly empty. In the ground floor hallway, we found fancy looking bicycles strapped tightly around a metal hand rail the building's proprietor had installed for just such a contingency. The place made us both think about college students. An apartment building filled with college students. Two floors up we found the apartment of the person who called in the report. It was a young couple, both males, who answered the door together.

They were in their twenties. One black. One white. Both *very* gay and proud of it. When the door opened, wafting out of the apartment's depths came this strong aroma of something being cooked that instantly made our mouths water. Whatever it was it smelled absolutely delicious.

"Oh my, it's the *police,* dear! Lord have mercy," the white guy said.

"Come in, officers. Come in. We *never* have visitors during the day. Do we, Howie?" the black guy answered.

"Never, dearie. Never," Howie replied. The two of them stepped back and made a path for us to enter. "Are you here because of our excited call to the dispatcher about the shooting we heard?"

"Or are you here because someone's complained we've been naughty again?" the black guy said, eyes twinkling, smiling, with dimples crackling across his cheeks angelically.

"'Bout the shooting," Frank grunted, narrowing his eyes and looking deeper into the apartment trying to eye the kitchen.

The white guy noticed. Glancing at his partner, he grinned impishly and winked. The black guy nodded, stepped in between Frank and I and grabbed an arm from each of us and began pulling us toward, apparently, the kitchen.

"Howie, where have our manners gone? Can't you see these two darling gentlemen are hungry?"

"Oh, goodie!" Howie exclaimed, clapping hands together eagerly, as he closed the door and raced for the kitchen. "I'm *sooo* excited!"

Turned out the two were students. Going to a very expensive school for Culinary Arts both Frank and I knew well. Howie Manning was the white guy. Eric Larry was the black guy. Both went to school on the G.I. bill. Get this—both had served in the Army together. As a sniper team. Eric had been the shooter. Howie his spotter. Three tours together in Afghanistan. Got out together—got married—and enrolled in the Culinary School immediately after their wedding and planned to open a restaurant the moment the graduated. If they could find the capital they needed.

Frank, the asshole, after finishing his third helping of something French made with a crab meat stuffed into a thick steak, young potatoes, and a delicious thick wine sauce over it all, gave me the critical eye but kept silent. I said nothing as I continued eating. I knew what he was thinking. But I had to admit it was astonishingly delicious.

We ate it all.

Didn't leave a spoonful of sauce for the two kids to lick up afterwards.

We apologized for our gluttony. Howie and Eric waved it off delightedly. They were very pleased we found their recent experiment so delicious. Eventually we got around to talking about what they saw and heard out in the cemetery behind their building.

The basic details were simple enough. The two came home from a late afternoon session at school. They walked into their hot apartment and began immediately opening windows to air the place out. That's when they heard the shooting.

"Nine millimeters, officers. Two of them. Off down by the creek in the cemetery," Eric nodded with certainty. Backed up with the knowing nod of Howie. "Plain as day. One shooting deliberately. The other rapid firing."

I started to ask if they were sure, but I didn't. Two Army snipers with three tours under their belts would know what a 9 millimeter sounded like.

"People plinking cans down by the creek?" Frank asked as we sat on the tall stools beside the small bar which separated the apartment's kitchen from its even smaller dining room.

"No no. Not this," Howie clucked, frowning and shaking his head. "We've heard that kind of shooting before. Someone was very angry at someone else. Very."

"Angry enough to kill darlings," Eric nodded. "But that's not all. When the shooting began, Howie and I went to the window to look out and possibly see something. You tell them, darling, what happened next."

"We were staring out toward the sound of the gunfire and this dark figure comes running out of the tree line—running as fast as he can go. More gun shots come out of the tree line. And then . . . and then . . . oh, *my*! I'm afraid you're not going to believe this."

"Christ, dear. *Tell* them. They'll believe us."

"Very well," sighed Howie, not looking convinced. "He disappeared, officers. Just . . . *disappeared* into thin air as he was running across the cemetery."

"Disappeared," I repeated, lifting an eyebrow in surprise. "He didn't fall down. A round didn't knock him down. He . . ."

"Simply vanished," Eric filled in, sounding absolutely certain.

Frank and I glanced at each other and then we looked at our hosts again.

"No," Eric said, shaking his head and holding up a hand to stop us. "I know what you're going to ask. The answer is no. We did not go to investigate. Howie and I have had our share of violence in our lives. More than enough, thank you. Guns and angry men and violence are not what we are about anymore."

"But we did call 911," Howie put in. "Twice. Once just after the man disappeared last night, and once this morning.

True enough. They had called in twice. The first time the dispatcher logged it but forgot to tell anyone about it. He figured like we did that someone was down by the creek target shooting. But the second time, a different dispatcher put a little more thought into it. So the note began making its way up through the channels until we decided to check it out.

We needed to check the cemetery out. We made our leave from the two budding chefs, seeing the concern in their eyes for our safety, and made our way out of the apartment building. Dancing through light traffic in front of the apartments, we climbed into the Camaro and slipped away from the curb. A half block down the street, there was a disused entrance into the rolling hills of the place. Underneath a bright summer's sun, the accumulated mass of headstones and sarcophagi thickly littering the almost virgin countryside on the southern edge of the city appeared picturesque.

But neither of us felt like admiring the scenery. The moment we rolled onto the white gravel single lane, which wound around the hills and dove in and out of small unseen meadows, we both felt it. That uneasiness most cops acquire from experience when something doesn't feel right. Rolling slowly down toward the creek, sitting in the open cockpit of the convertible, we both reached for our weapons at the same time.

We parked the car in the shade of a large oak tree and climbed out slowly. Our eyes taking in the immediate surroundings suspiciously. Today, I was experimenting. Instead of the trusty Kimber .45 caliber I generally wore in a shoulder holster underneath my armpit, I was toting around a Smith & Wesson .40 caliber M&P. Less weight and more rounds than the trusty Kimber. The Kimber held eight rounds of .45 cal. ACP. The Smith & Wesson held 15 rounds of the .40 caliber. Big difference if you ever found yourself in a fire fight. As Frank and I stood beside the Camaro eyeing the thick trees surrounding us, each of us gripping our weapons firmly in hand, the idea of a few extra rounds in the ammo clip sounded good to me.

We found the body about fifteen minutes later, lying face down in an open grave. Interestingly, he had been shot high in the left shoulder as he was running away from the shooter. But his death was someone coming along and bashing the back of his head in with something. Like maybe the bloody shovel thrown into the grave that was lying in the dirt beside him.

The odd thing was there was only one set of footprints leading to the grave. Those being the long strides of a man running. The victim's. No one else had disturbed the loose soil until Frank and I came up to the grave and looked in.

Frank scowled, said something to himself, and looked up at me.

"Ghosts. I hate ghosts."

"Yeah. Me too, buddy. But the question to be asked is *why*? Why his death? Why here? What's going on?"

"Let's backtrack," the big guy growled, turning partially and pointing the barrel of his Glock 17 back to the Camaro. "He came running from that direction. So he must have seen something over there."

We retraced our steps, found the prints of the dead man running toward his grave, and followed them back past the car and into the dry creek bottom. We lost the tracks as we slipped through the thick underbrush but picked them up in a couple of places in the dry creek bed. Still running. The guy was running for his life down the rocky creek bed. Whatever spooked him had done so a few yards up stream. Gripping our weapons firmly, we began moving in that direction.

That's when it started happening. The spooky stuff.

Like I said, neither Frank nor I believe in ghosts. But that's not saying there have not been a few times in our professional careers where odd things have happened to both of us which we've found hard to explain. Like this case. Moving across the rough rocks of the creek bed, we began hearing sounds. Sounds like branches of low hanging trees and brush rattling after something large had slipped past them surreptitiously. A soft sound like a hand held fan sweeping across the cloth of a bed spread. And then there were small rocks, rocks about the size of marbles, rattling down the banks of the creek and into the creek itself.

The sounds were sudden. Unexpected. And they happened each time we were looking away in a different direction.

Once, I thought I saw something in the corner of my eye flash for a nanosecond into the opening between two large trees before disappearing into the gloomy darkness of the underbrush. Something brown. Like a deer's flank. Or maybe someone wearing chaps.

In front of me, Frank bent down lower, turned to look at me, and placed a finger up to his lips, warning me to keep quiet. I nodded. Ahead of us, I heard the faint sounds of people talking, along with the sound of someone hard at work with a shovel. Someone was digging rapidly and hurriedly, dumping the shovel loads to one side. Behind Frank still, we began moving toward the sound.

That's when all hell broke loose.

Behind us and standing on the high bank of the creek on the right side, there was a sudden loud screech, which sounded like someone in immense pain, just before the thundering explosion of an AK-47 went off on full auto, booming across the cemetery. I whirled, bringing the Smith & Wesson up at the same time, and briefly caught sight of something in a tannish/brown buckskin dancing around in a macabre little ditty before disappearing back into the underbrush. But when it did, a man suddenly appeared from the underbrush, sliding down the loose gravel of the creek bank, his head lopped unnaturally to one side and quite dead. Someone, or *something*, had broken the man's neck like it was a twig and let him go.

But there was no time to go over and examine the body. Suddenly, the dark underworld and still air of the creek bottom lit up with heavy gunfire. In less than a second, Frank and I found ourselves in a war zone. We both dived for whatever cover we could find, firing away at unseen targets as we did. For maybe five seconds, the noise of open urban warfare rang loud and clear. Once I caught sight of someone holding an AR-15 in his hands and blazing away in our direction. Two rounds in the man's left leg brought him dropping into the dry creek bed screaming in pain.

And then—as suddenly as it started—it was over.

Silence. Sweeping across the semi-darkness of the creek with a startling clarity.

But not absolute silence. Above us, on either side, hidden in the underbrush, we could hear the groans of several men in deep pain. And then, there was the rattling of underbrush to our left. Loud. Unnerving. And then . . . silence.

Glancing behind me, I saw Frank was still in one piece and functioning. Turning, looking up at the creek banks, I wondered what was going to happen next. We both scanned the banks and then began moving up and out of the creek bed. As we gained the line of underbrush above us, the voices of Howie and Eric began yelling at the top of their lungs.

"Sergeant Hahn! Sergeant Morales! Can you hear us? Help is one the way! We've called the police and told them you need immediate help! Ambulances are on the way!"

The two were some yards behind us. So we heard them first before we heard the approaching sirens of a dozen or more police cars heading in our direction. In ten minutes, the creek bed and cemetery were filled with police officers from three different local departments.

It was drug related. A cartel used a particular grave site, which they could reach by tunneling from the creek into the grave itself, to store the cache of drugs brought up from Mexico. They would park their truck a few hundred yards down from the grave, trek down the dry creek bed until they came to the designated site, and then dig into the creek bank.

Turned out, the dead man lying face down in the open grave we found was one of the cartel members. One of the survivors of the fire fight had witnessed the sudden flight of the man running away the day before. The boss of the gang thought the guy was running out on them and so chased him down and shot him in the back. The guy fell in the open grave. But that was it. After the guy fell in the grave the boss turned around and walked back to his crew to finish the job. The witness swears no one bashed the guy in the head with a shovel. Why would they? Everyone thought he was already dead.

Never found out who killed the guy. We also never found out who had swept mostly unseen through the creek's thick foliage and devastated the drug gang in silent hand to hand combat, saving Frank and mine's keesters in the process.

Our first suspicions naturally flowed toward Howie and Eric. Ex-combat veterans. Trained in close hand to hand combat and good at it. When we found them standing beside the Camaro, looking worried and tired from sprinting down from the apartment building and across the open cemetery to the edge of the creek, neither one was dressed in anything of tannish leather. One had on a blue paisley silk shirt and a pair of blue jeans. The other wore something in lime green with a pair of off white shorts. They swore they had no hand in saving our lives.

It was hard not to believe them.

So.

Frank and I still do not believe in ghosts. But we haven't a clue as to what happened in that creek bottom that day. All I can tell you is this. About five months later, Frank and I each became one/quarter owners of a very chic restaurant, which opened in the heart of the downtown district by two fabulous chefs.

Yes—don't remind me. It takes all kinds of people, fella. All kinds.

5

THE CURIOUS MR. KLAUS

The holidays.

The constant blare of Christmas carols.

The hordes of people moving like gigantic herds of cattle from one store to the next in search of that elusive cut-throat sale. Exiting stores so loaded down with packages that they're bent over and staggering from the load.

The holidays.

Everyone supposed to be in a gay, happy mood. The Spirit of Joy and Giving. The Holiday Spirits. And other crappy emotions like this.

Sure. Uh huh.

And of course, the weather in this town contributing to the holiday mood. Frigid cold winds blowing off the rivers—cold enough to make a space probe setting on Mars surveying orange skies seem like a tropical paradise. And snow about every other day. Coming down with a vengeance and screwing up the city's traffic in one gigantic snarl of howling cars, profane-laced drivers, and terminal cases of ill-tempered assholes.

It was eight in the evening on Christmas Eve night, and only Frank and I—and the lieutenant—were on duty.

The holidays. I hate them.

"Ah, quit bitching ya mumbling ole' Grinch. Here—drink this. Some eggnog with a little spice in it ought to make you feel better."

Frank—my partner here in Homicide down in the South Side Precinct—lumbered over to me like an uncaged gorilla and shoved a tall glass of yellow liquid into my hand. As tall as me, but he was maybe fifty pounds heavier. The glass of 'nog in his mitt for a hand looked like a shot glass to any other normal human being. Keeping my opinion to myself, I lifted the glass and took a long pull from it.

And almost gagged from the amount of alcohol in it.

"Jesus, what did you do? Drain the anti-freeze on your kid's snowmobile? Fer chrissakes don't light a match in here. The whole miserable place will be blown sky high!"

"It's good, huh?" Frank answered, the corners of his lips twitching—his way of grinning—as he sat down at his desk and looked at me. "It must be pretty good. Yank's been over here eight times to ask for more."

Yank was Lieutenant Dimitri Yankovich. Second shift watch commander and directly in charge of the precinct's second floor—the detective section of the precinct. Yank was a good man. A great boss. He rarely had anything cross to say to anyone. And apparently he liked Frank's eggnog. A lot.

"Got any more?" I asked, looking down at the empty glass and then back at my partner.

Frank pointed to the ancient, battered, scarred relic of what once had been a refrigerator in the janitor's room over by the stairwell. I turned and started to make my way to it, but the phone on my desk lit up. The square little light aglow on the phone told me the call was from downstairs, from the booking desk. Reaching for it, I threw it to my ear and kept it in place with a shoulder as I pulled the chair out of my desk and started to sit down.

"Yes, Dougie? Whatta ya got?"

Dougie was Sergeant Douglas Timmons. A twenty-five year veteran of the uniformed force—of which half of it was sitting behind the booking desk and listening to just about every kind of crime, every crazy and loony bin tale, a human being could commit. He'd seen it all and cleaned up most of the messes left behind. Nothing got under his cool. Nothing surprised him.

"I'm sending up an elderly gentleman by the name of Friedrich Klaus. He owns Klaus' Tailoring over on Houston Street. For the last two days he's been coming in here asking to see you, Turner. You're here. He's here. It's time for you to hear his story."

"What's it about?"

"Naw—not going to say. If I did you'd probably have me committed to a funny farm. It's your squawk, kid. And it's a doosey."

I told him to send him up and glanced at Frank.

"Customers?"

"Elves," I said, turning to look at the stairwell and the soon to arrive Friedrich Klaus. "Who else would be out on a night like this?"

Sonofabitch. Elves indeed.

The little man came up the stairs to the squad room dressed in a derby, carrying an umbrella, and wearing a very well made heavy navy blue trench coat. He had bright, ruddy cheeks, a round and very red nose, wore wire-rim spectacles and had an expertly trimmed and maintained white beard and mustache— the whitest beard and mustache I had ever seen. Glancing at

Frank, I lifted an eyebrow questioningly. He shrugged gently, mouthing "Elves" silently to me.

"Detectives Hahn and Morales, at last I have the pleasure of meeting you!"

His handshake was surprisingly strong through the gray colored gloves he wore. I asked him to sit down and tell us what was so important to come out into a night like this and drive through the wind and snow to come to South Side Precinct.

The little man with the ruddy fat cheeks nodded, but the merriment illuminating his eyes switched off like a light bulb and was replaced with a deep look of concern.

"I'm afraid we must set aside pleasantries, gentlemen. You two are the only ones who can help me. And we have so little time."

"What can we do for you?" I asked, sitting down at my desk and swiveling the chair around to look at the nattily dressed little man.

"Tomorrow night, precisely at nine p.m., I am going to die. Unless—unless you can find the madman who is going to kill me."

Frank and I stared at the little man in front of us—blinking a couple of times in surprise—unable to find anything to say. The ruddy faced man sitting across from us first looked at me, then at Frank, the irritation on his face clearly visible.

"I see things, boys. I have . . . visions. Glimpses of people . . . events . . . places. Sometimes they are quite vivid. Sometimes they are fuzzy. Like watching a television show through wax paper. I also feel other people's thoughts. I feel the thoughts coming out of both of you right now. You think I'm crazy."

"You feel thoughts?" I repeated. "Not read thoughts. But feel thoughts. There's a difference?"

"Very much so," the little elf nodded, frowning. "I never hear exactly what a person is thinking. But I get an overall impression. Like the one coming from you, Sergeant Morales. You want proof. Solid proof to back up what I say. Very well, try this for size."

Mister Klaus suddenly stood up, turned, and made a bee line straight to the janitor's room where the squad room's fridge sat. He moved as if he knew exactly where he was going. Even though, to my knowledge, he had never stepped into this building before. When he came out of the room he had the big pitcher of Frank's eggnog in his gloved hand. Walking to where we were sitting, he poured each of us a full glass—and one for himself with a clean glass he pulled off the shelf above the fridge.

"The rum in the eggnog you made, Sergeant Morales. It's from the bottle of expensive rum Sergeant Hahn bought for you and has hidden above the hat rack over there. He's going to give it to you tonight when the shift is over. But you found it when you two came on duty this afternoon. So you decided to make some of your famous brew. Quite delicious, I might add."

Startled, I looked at the big guy sitting across from me. Frank was looking at me, the corners of his lips twitching—laughter in his eyes. He nodded, shrugged, and reached for his eggnog.

"And you, Sergeant Hahn. You're thinking about buying an old car to restore for your car collection. An Oldsmobile 442 is it? Well, look in your 'In Box' and see what the motor vehicle department says about it. Second piece of paper in the box. Yes. That's the one."

I was thinking about buying an old muscle car to rebuild. That's what I do for a hobby. Frowning, I pulled the report out of the In Box and glanced at it. Stolen. Stolen in '86 off a residential street in San Diego.

Grinning—impressed—I tossed the report onto the desk and brought my attention back to our elf.

"Who's trying to kill you?"

"I don't know. But apparently he knows the two of you. He really wants to kill either you, Sergeant Hahn, or you, Sergeant Morales. I don't know precisely. But he's using me to get to you."

"Huh," I grunted, frowning and pulling on the lobe of my right ear. "That would mean he somehow knows you and knows of your . . . ah . . . clairvoyant gifts."

"What do you see . . . or feel . . . from his thoughts?" Frank asked.

"Shoes," he whispered for a reply.

"Shoes," I echoed, frowning.

"For the last week I've . . . I've been catching these mental glimpses of tomorrow night's event. Images of a metal pole and street signs—trees behind the signs blowing from a strong wind —snow falling out the trees in a white curtain—an old, abandoned house. But the most frightening image I see is a dim, partially lit hallway with a pair of a man's legs, dressed in gray slacks, lying in the hallway with a stream of blood flowing past his right leg. That's where the shoes come in. Black loafers, made by a small firm called Pakkers. Very rare. Hard to find."

I arched an eyebrow in surprise. On my feet were a pair of black loafers. The very brand our little elf mentioned. Throwing a look down at his feet, I noticed he had the same style of shoes on as well.

I glanced at Frank. He was watching me closely. A frown on his thin, gray lips.

"You see my conundrum," the ruddy faced, bearded, little tailor said softly. "One of us is going to die, Sergeant Hahn. I'm thinking it will be me. But it could very well be you."

"The street signs. Where?" asked Frank.

"Corner of Dreary Lane and Hope Streets."

I would have grinned and dismissed the whole thing as a

hoax—maybe a stunt perpetrated by a partner whom I knew liked to pull tricky little pranks on people. On me in particular. But there *was* a Dreary Lane. And a Hope Street. And they did cross each other. Frank's ugly mug wasn't grinning that devilish little grin he almost had on his lips when he was pulling something on me. He looked deadly serious. Our little elf looked pale and scared.

"Okay. Tell you what," I said, nodding. "Frank and I will go over to Dreary Lane and Hope and check it out. I want you to stay right here. Downstairs. The desk sergeant will keep an eye on you until we return. Understand?"

It didn't take long to drive across town and find the corner of Dreary Lane and Hope. Curiously, half way there, the wind picked up and started blowing strong enough to send sheets of snow sailing across the streets in a white curtain. Climbing out of our car, I glanced up at the street corner. The paint on the street sign for Dreary Lane was peeling off. It was half coated with a thick smear of dark red rust. Like the color of blood. Reaching up, I pulled the collar of my heavy wool Navy P-coat up and hunkered down in it. The wind was freezing cold.

"Turner," Frank's voice said calmly. "Look at the trees."

Behind the street signs, the trees were dancing madly. Snow was falling rapidly out of them, creating a blinding curtain of pure white. One look at the trees and the snow and my hand reached inside my coat, my fingers wrapping around the butt of the .45 caliber Kimber semi-automatic riding underneath my left armpit.

I dunno—but have you ever had chills walk their icy fingers up and down your spine? Chills not from the cold or the wind. But from something else. Something like—dread.

Sitting on a small knoll was an empty two-story house. The house out of the Hitchcock movie *Psycho* came to mind. Dark, lifeless windows stared at us. Window shutters somewhere on the second floor banged against the house thanks to the wind. Directly above the main entrance, there was a busted window with a single, faded white curtain, which waved at us as we approached. Walking through the deep snow up to the house, I heard Frank grunt beside me.

"I'm not wrong am I? I mean . . . this is Christmas, isn't it? Not Halloween?"

I grinned and moved onto the porch and tried the front door to see if it was locked with a gloved hand. It wasn't. We searched the house from the attic down to the basement and found nothing, but twice we both thought we heard footsteps walking across the floor above our heads. And once—faintly— I thought I heard laughter. Still—we couldn't be sure. The wind was even stronger outside and blowing through the house like a small tornado. The footsteps, the laughter—it could have been just the wind and our nerves playing tricks on us.

But I didn't think so.

When we got back to South Side our Friedrich Klaus was missing. Gone. He had told Sergeant Timmons he was going home to wrap some Christmas presents. If we had any questions we knew where to find him.

"Turner, tomorrow is Christmas. The wife and kids and I are driving down to Kansas City to have Christmas with my brother and his family. I won't be around until well past midnight."

"I know, Frank. I know. Don't worry about it. I'm doing nothing but just hanging out at my place. I'll take care of this. It's probably nothing anyway. Say hello to your brother and his wife for me."

Christmas.

A time of cheer. Of exchanging gifts with loved ones. Of watching children's faces light up as they open their presents.

Of laughing and telling old family stories around the dining room table while relaxing after the big Christmas dinner.

Christmas.

I sat in my car across the street from the house of our curious Mr. Klaus. Sat behind the wheel of the '66 Pontiac GTO and ate hamburgers and drank coke as I watched the snow come in off the Brown River. Nothing moved down the quiet street of the Klaus' house. Kids came out late in the afternoon with new sleds and tried them out in the blizzard and threw snowballs at anything that moved. A couple of cabs plowed their way through the streets to come to a halt in front of a house or two. Grandparents and friends climbed out, carrying bags of brightly covered Christmas packages with them. They were greeted half way up the snow covered sidewalks by friends and family who poured out of their houses to envelop them with glad tidings.

At a little past eight p.m., the garage door to the Klaus' house opened and a bright red, four wheel drive Jeep Cherokee pulled out, smashed through the wall of snow which had built up in front of the garage, and backed into the street. Our ruddy complexioned elf was sitting behind the Jeep's wheel.

I wasn't surprised in the least when the red Jeep made its slow way across the deserted streets of the city and came to a halt in front of a house setting on the corner of Dreary Lane and Hope Streets. I watched Klaus roll out of his car and make his way through the snow to enter the house. The moment he disappeared inside, I climbed out of the GTO and started toward the back door of the creepy place.

Coming in through the kitchen door, gun in one hand, and a big six-cell Mag light in the other, I moved through the kitchen and entered a long dark hall which led to the living room. Stepping into the living room, I heard a squeak of flooring behind me. Turning, I just had a glimpse of a black mass flashing toward me, a hand rising up and over his head, something thick and black in his gloved hand.

It was a crowbar. It cracked across my gun hand in a searing blow. I heard bones snapping like match sticks. Staggering back, I threw the Mag light up and made the second blow of the crowbar glance off and away from my skull. But in the darkness, I didn't see the gloved fist in time. It caught me in the jaw, snapping my head back and exploding bright lights in my head. I don't remember dropping to my knees from the blow. Shaking my head, trying to get some vision back, I tried to stand up. But my legs felt like led weights and I couldn't focus my eyes.

Laughter—I heard laughter—that of a madman's, and then —and then—through the pain . . .

BOOM! BOOM!

The ringing explosions of a 9 mm Glock exploding in two rapid shots directly behind me. I heard a grunt and then the clatter of a heavy body falling to the floor in front of me.

When I opened my eyes and blinked, I found myself in a sitting position. Braced in a sitting position by the snow shovel sized paw of Frank kneeling beside me. My right arm felt like someone had parked a bull dozer on it and was trying to grind it to pieces with its tracks. I couldn't open my jaw too much. But my eyes were working. I could see the carrot colored hair and the square jaw of Frank as he held me firmly in place.

"You okay, Turn? Never mind. Stay still. Got an ambulance crew on the way. And don't move that right arm of yours. Dammit boy, but you look like hell."

I grinned.

"Hiya, pal. How's the brother and his brood?"

"Boring. As they usually are. The fucker never changes."

I looked toward the semi-lit hallway. Lying in a puddle of dim light were a set of legs. Dressed in gray slacks—feet covered with a pair of black Pakkers. Blood flowed like cold molasses on the floor past his right leg.

"Klaus?"

"Not Klaus," Frank grunted, shaking his head. "Haven't a clue who he is. But I know Friedrich Klaus. He spends his Christmas with his son down in Florida every year. Apparently this fucker didn't know that."

"You knew all the time he wasn't a tailor?" I asked looking up in the darkness at the dim outline of Frank's face.

"Yes. Thought I'd let him play it out and see where this went. Farther than I wanted it to. Sorry, buddy."

"Well, just to let you know. You're buying lunch for the rest of the year," I growled. "Still. I'm glad you showed up."

Christmas. A time to be with family. A time to enjoy good cheer and the laughter from good friends. But—did I say how much I hated Christmas?

Not this one. This one I was happy to be alive.

6

GLEAMING BLADES OF JADE

The red Shelby Mustang slid up beside an empty street
curb and came to a halt in the deep shadows between
two unlit street lights. Cutting the engine switch and pulling
the keys, the Ford V8's deep rumble ceased abruptly, and in the
process, the night became very quiet and oddly menacing.
Climbing out of the recently restored Shelby, the bright red
paint so fresh and clean one could see starlight reflecting off the
hood, I glanced at my partner and then turned to stare at what
was in front of us.

It was a hot night. In late July.

Sure, cities in late summer are hot at night. But summer
heat in this city is like no other. Humidity thick enough to
squeeze water out of the air with your bare hands. The nagging
line of growing panic that maybe you were about to suffocate
with each breath you took. The physical effort it took just to
walk across the cement pavement and sidewalks with the coils
of radiating heat rolling out in pulsating waves of strength-
sapping intensity.

When it got this hot and clammy you could bet on one

thing. Static electricity filled the night with the promise of a thunderstorm. A big one. Filled with lightning and rolling thunder that would start sometime after midnight and roll on until just before dawn.

Like clockwork, brother. Like taxes.

The storm was coming and there wasn't a damn thing you could do about it. Except endure. Except sit inside someplace dry with a bucket of ice filled with about a half dozen bottles of cold beer in it to pass the time. 'Cause you sure as hell wouldn't get any sleep. Not tonight. Not with the light show, pounding rain, and window clattering constant roll of thunder keeping you up.

And here we were, my partner and I, about to start working another homicide case.

The call came in at a quarter to midnight, fifteen minutes before Frank and I were going off duty. Yeah, typical. We were the only detectives available. Everyone else was out working cases. Out of the four precinct houses, it's a relatively small city, so we're nothing like a New York or Kansas City—we were the only homicide detectives available. So there we were. In a cemetery situated on a high bluff overlooking the dark waters of the wide Brown river. Facing the open wrought iron entrance gates of the cemetery and observing, off in the distance, the weaving and bobbing beams of flashlights of the two patrol unit officers who had responded first to the call.

"I'm not getting any positive vibes about this one, Turner. Really bad Juju here. Nothing positive at all."

I cracked a smirk and glanced at my partner.

"Frank, I didn't know. You're superstitious?"

"You know better than that. But you feel it too. And don 't deny it."

Actually, I did feel it.

When you've been working homicide cases as long as we

have you develop a sixth sense. It's something like the sensation of creepy crawly things moving about in the back of your mind. It doesn't happen often. It's not common. But brother, I'm telling you, when the creepy crawlies start acting up, you'd better pay attention. It's an early warning sign letting you know things are not what they appear to be.

Like the beginning of this case.

The moment we pulled up in front of the iron gates, the warning lights began blinking. A dead body in a cemetery. Almost a cliché. A dead body in a cemetery with fog beginning to roll in off the river. Flashlight beams from the uniforms who arrived first jerked back and forth across the cemetery stones and then focused back into sharp definition as they walked around the body looking for evidence. By the time we got to the murder scene, all the uniforms were concentrated in one tight pack, their flashlights aimed down at something lying on a grave beside the body.

We looked at the body. Both of us were expecting the worse. Kinda comes automatically if you're going out to a murder scene in the middle of a graveyard. We weren't disappointed. The deceased was a male in his late twenties or early thirties. Someone had used some kind of rough woven rope and tied the victim's hands behind his back. An odd looking piece of cloth was used as a gag. The cloth looked old. Dirty. Like something one would pull out of a trash heap. Or maybe an archeological site.

But there was no doubt about the cause of death. Our killer had opened the man's chest up from chin to navel and cut the man's heart out. The heart was missing. But lying on the grave beside him was the instrument used for the grisly deed. A knife. A knife made of two stones. The blade was a long, wide thing of black obsidian. The handle was made of green jade.

Green jade carved into the image of a large hunting cat curling down, about to take a leap at its victim.

"Quaint," Frank grunted succinctly as he held his flashlight beam solidly on the middle of the dead man's chest. "Cause of death couldn't be a gunshot wound, or a baseball bat, or even a chainsaw. Oh hell no. Has to be an Aztec warrior's blade. A somewhat dull one at that."

I held the flashlight in my hand aimed at the knife. Kneeling, I studied the blade a little closer. The weapon was covered in blood. But the handle looked as if someone had used something to wipe it clean. Clean of any prints undoubtedly. But the weapon looked old and genuine.

"The Jaguar is a common motif for the Aztec. A number of warrior societies within the Aztec Empire used it as their main symbol," my walking encyclopedia of a partner growled. He didn't sound pleased. "And yes, before you ask. They practiced human sacrifice."

I stood up and took a step back as a crime lab specialist stepped in and began taking a number of different shots of the body with his big digital camera. I turned to the left and saw Flattery and O'Connor, the two uniformed officers who first arrived on the scene, walking toward us.

"'The body been identified?"

"His driver license says his name is Peter Silvers. Lives over in the Oak Tree apartments off of Simpson Road. He was forty two years old. For the moment that's all we know."

There was just the suggestion of a third generation Irish lilt in Flattery's voice. Three generations of Irish cops. Yes, I know. An obvious cliché. But that's the way it was.

"We sent a patrol unit over to the address to check it out," O'Connor put in, aiming the beam of his flashlight at the dead figure on the ground. "Holy Mary. Someone did not like this boyo one bit. Hell of a way to go, sergeant. Hell of a way to go."

Frank and I both nodded. We're both sergeants. Detective sergeants in Homicide. The four of us—Frank and myself plus the uniforms, Flattery and O'Connor—have worked more homicide cases than we care to remember. We were all old friends. Family.

"The grounds are clean, boys. We've gone over the place twice with a comb. Our victim and his killer came in through the gate yonder and the killing happened right here," Flattery spoke up again, the beam of his flashlight twisting and dodging around like a Jedi light saber. "No prints of any kind. No footprints. No tire tracks. No sign of a struggle. Just a lot of the victim's blood and that damn knife."

I nodded and turned the beam of my flashlight toward my partner's feet. He stood across from the body looking down at the bright screen of his smart phone. As I glanced at him, I saw an eyebrow go up on his forehead.

"Hey, Turn. Look at this."

He reached across the body with an outstretched arm and handed me his phone. I took the phone and glanced at it. There was a big story splashed across it. A big story about a recent discovery in South America.

Doctor Peter Silvers, head of the Archeological Department at Anderson University, recently returned from a dig in Guatemala after he and his team spent six grueling months in a South American jungle. He and his team of archeological students discovered a new Aztec city deep in the jungles of Guatemala. This news has set the archeological world on fire since the Aztec Empire centered around the high plateaus of Central and Western Mexico. An Aztec city deep in the jungles of Guatemala promises to start an intense debate in the archeological world as to the size and importance of the

Aztec Empire, with Dr. Silvers at the heart of the controversy.

"Where do you want to go first? His apartment or the university?" the big guy asked.

I grinned and shot him a questioning glance.

"Why do I have to make the decision? We're equal in rank. We've been on the force the same length of time. You could be the lead investigator on this and I could be the side kick for once."

"Nope," the answer came back in the dark. "Being a side kick is an important role in our social dynamic which requires a certain subtle handling. A talent which, I'm afraid, you are sorely lacking."

"Are you saying I can't be . . . uh . . . as subtle as you?" I asked, grinning.

I once saw Frank punch a fist through a cement block wall. Literately. One punch. Made a hole two feet wide. Another time I saw him bend over and look at a drug lord in the face. Nose to nose. Didn't say a word to the guy in the interrogation room. Not one word. The guy pissed his pants. Ran down his right leg and made a big yellow puddle on the floor underneath his chair.

Yeah. He's that kind of guy. Subtle.

About as subtle as a fracken' Main Battle Tank setting in the middle of a Tupperware party. That kind of subtle.

"I'm saying your talent is that of the traditional hero mythos. With a movie star face like that, the news cameras and women just swoon over you. Looks like that make all the questions come to you first. Or, if the case goes belly-up and down the toilet, all the shit slaps you in the face first. I kinda like that last part, buddy. Really like it."

Okay, I look like a dead man. A movie actor out of the 30's

who was fairly well known. Curly black hair, black mustache, a smirk on my chops that never goes away. Dimples in the cheeks. The works. Yes. Whenever we are forced to stand in front of a bunch of reporters, the questions come to me first. Yes. When an investigation goes south—flushes down the toilet as Frank defined it—I'm the one that tries to get us out of the dog house.

Sighing, grinning, and shaking my head, I didn't say a thing but waved a hand at him and started off through the darkness toward the car. Half way across the cemetery my cellphone rang.

"Sergeant, this is Malone. We're over at the dead man's apartment. You two had better get over here as fast as you can. There's something you gotta see for yourself."

We climbed into the Shelby and drove across a semi-deserted city. The night was still extremely hot. But still. No wind. No movement at all. Lightning filled the near horizon. The storm was almost upon us. And it was going to pour like a 'sumbitch.

Like a fracken' biblical deluge.

I just hoped we were inside somewhere when it came. Drowning while standing up on our feet didn't sound very appealing to me.

Officer Stan Malone and his partner Officer Eddie Driskel were waiting for us in the apartment door of the dead man's apartment. Both looked about as pale as a humans can get while still being considered alive. Both were young patrol cops with not too much experience underneath their belts, so I can understand why they looked the way they did when we walked in.

The dead man's pet dog was dead. Dead and pinned to the floor in the middle of the living room in some kind of ritual killing rite. Beside the bloody body was a stone knife, an exact replica of the one we found beside Dr. Silvers' body in the cemetery. Smeared on the wall was the dog's blood in a strange pictographic language I vaguely recognized.

"As you might suspect," my know-it-all partner drawled out sarcastically, "Aztec. Actually, a variation of traditional Aztec. Maybe original Nahual. Or a Mayan derivative."

I looked at Frank incredulously. Sure. I knew the guy was smart. I knew he had an eidetic memory. I knew that in the fifteen or so years we'd worked together I'd never stumped him with any of my esoteric, only-the-gods-could-possibly-know questions. But this was too much.

"How in hell could you possibly know the difference between Aztec and Mayan writing, you big goof. And don't tell me you read it in a book, or I swear to god I'm gonna hit you with that lamp over there!"

Frank stood beside me, the corners of his lips twitching, and shrugged his shoulders as he looked me straight in the eye.

"I read a book," he said dryly.

I reached for the lamp—but stopped in mid motion when something behind us and to our left thumped loudly on a closed door. We pulled our weapons from our shoulder holsters and cautiously approached the door. I nodded to Frank and reached for the door knob and threw the door open without offering much of a target to anyone on the other side. Frank, gun up in front of his face, gave me cover as I stepped cautiously to one side and peeked into the room.

She was lying on the carpet of the bedroom, her feet bound with rope but only inches away from the door sill. Her arms were pulled back behind her and tied with a rope as well. She was down to her bra and underwear lying on the floor. And bleeding. Bleeding profusely from a deep knife wound that started just below her throat and ran across her upper chest to just above the sternum.

In the bedroom, lying on the floor, were her clothes. The

round bed looked rumpled and filled with bloodstains. On the far side of the room a set of French doors leading out onto the apartment's balcony were wide open. The black rectangle of the night on the other side of the French doors spasmodically flashed with bright lightning. I glanced at Frank, who nodded and holstered his weapon as he bent down to apply some first aid to the bleeding wound of the woman. I nodded, turned, and ran toward the open balcony doors and out into the night.

Not too far off, the rumble of the approaching storm filled the hot night air as I began looking for our quarry. A dark flash of motion to my left caught my attention. Lifting my weapon I turned and saw something impossible. Simply impossible.

A black silhouette of a human form was leaping from one apartment balcony to the next in a stepladder fashion, descending one floor at a time with each daring leap into the darkness. Three leaps. That's all it took. On the fourth leap into the darkness I heard him grunt as he landed on the sidewalk running parallel with the apartment building. One running step to his right and he simply disappeared into the darkness. Just dissolved into nothing.

I stood on the balcony for a few seconds in disbelief and then, automatically, shoved the .45 caliber Kimber back into the shoulder holster and walked back into the well-lit apartment bedroom behind me. As I walked past the round bed in the middle of the bedroom carpet, I noticed the bloody sheets. They were soaked in blood. More blood than the woman had had time to deposit. Soaked more than what Peter Silvers could have leaked out. Frowning, I moved past the bed and knelt down opposite Frank and looked at the sacrificial entity we just saved from a gruesome death.

"Her name is Maria Gomez. She's one of Dr. Silvers' archeological students he took with him down to Guatemala."

"Did she say anything about who did this to her?"

"Just mentioned a name before she passed out from the loss of blood. She said 'Mictlan.'"

"Mictlan," I echoed, frowning. "The Aztec version of Hell isn't it?"

Frank nodded as he stood up from kneeling beside the unconscious woman. In the distance we heard the wailing of sirens approaching, one of them being an ambulance. We looked down at Maria Gomez. She was a lucky kid. We interrupted her would-be-killer as he was about to carve her living heart out of her chest. There would be one ugly scar to remind her of the terror she must have went through in trying to fight off her assailant. But a scar was better than being dead. A scar was something you could learn to live with. But dead was, well —*permanent*.

We helped load the woman onto the medic's gurney and then into the ambulance. After that we went looking. Looking for a way to tie one murder and one attempted murder with the word Mictlan. It didn't take long.

His name was Arturo Ochero Mitclan Gomez.

The brother of Maria Gomez. The middle child in a family of eight. The one brother who had been diagnosed as homicidally insane while a young teenager and committed to an insane asylum just outside of Mexico City. The reason for his commitment was a story in itself.

Apparently, the boy had a fondness for getting lost in the jungles for days on end. One time he disappeared for two weeks before emerging. When he returned to his family's estates, it was apparent his personality had changed dramatically and dangerously. He claimed he was an Aztec prince, and the gods demanded the youngest daughter in the family had to be sacrificed to them in the sacrificial rites of the ancients. Maria Gomez happened to be the youngest daughter in the family. Twice he tried to carve her up with some old stone knifes he found in the jungles. Twice he was stopped.

After the second attempt, the family decided to send him away. He was supposed to have been permanently assigned to a hospital for the criminally insane.But bad financial times in Mexico forced the hospital to close. But before Maria's family found another safe place for her sick brother, Arturo Ochero Mitclan Gomez disappeared. Fled southward into the jungles of Central America and was never heard from again.

Until an American led archeological crew spent six months in a Guatemalan jungle hunting for a long lost Aztec city.

We gleaned this information after calling Maria's parents in Mexico. They told us the whole story and warned us the son was no one to dismiss. The boy truly believed he was an Aztec warrior-prince and was very good with those stone knives he always carried with him. The parents informed us two of their older children were flying up as quickly as arrangements could be made. They were going to take Maria back to Mexico as soon as she was able to be transported home.

At the end of our conversation, they told us to be careful. Since we interrupted the killing ceremony, in Arturo's eyes, one, if not both of us, would have to die in a gesture of atonement for our sins.

We looked for Arturo. He was like a ghost. He simply vanished into the night.

To say the least, when we finally decided to call it quits and I drove Frank to his house in the suburbs before going to downtown to my place, the drive across town was filled with gloomy silence. As I watched Frank crawl out of the Shelby and walk up to his house it started to rain. Rain drops splattered across the windshield in a kind of polite warning, but just as the front porch light to Frank's house lit up and his wife opened the door to greet him, the rain came down in buckets. Big buckets.

Water everywhere. In a matter of seconds it was raining so hard I barely could see the end of the Shelby's hood in front of me as I pulled away from the curb.

The drive back to the brick warehouse turned condo I owned downtown was a combination of driving and motoring, like a yacht through flooded streets. Make that rivers. Yes. It was that kind of rain.

When I rolled into the ground floor span of dry cement that used to be an old automotive repair shop and parked in an empty slot between two other muscle cars I owned, all I could think about was getting some sleep. Frank and I had put in close to eighteen hours. We were both exhausted. A hot shower and an empty bed sounded good to me as I started up the wooden stairs, heading for the apartment situated over the ground floor garage.

Half way up the stairs I wasn't tired anymore. Something had changed my mind.

To fill in some blanks here, maybe I should tell you I collect American made muscle cars for a hobby. I collect them and rebuild them myself. I own an old brick warehouse down close to the Brown River as my residence. The upstairs loft I turned into my living quarters. The ground floor downstairs is where I store the cars and rebuild them. As I climbed up the stairs toward the apartment there were eight cars setting on the cement floor of the garage below me. Seven fully restored. The eighth partially restored.

A rather hefty inheritance gave me the wherewithal to do all this. Yeah, some say I'm rich. I guess I am. But that's neither here nor there. I'm still the same cop I was *before* I inherited a boatload of money.

All this is relevant because, when I took over the building, I thought about putting an elevator in and removing the stairs altogether. I decided I liked the old stairs and forgot about the elevator. It was the stairs which saved my life that night. The stairs and the rain.

When I entered the apartment, I walked through the dark dining room toward the kitchen, flipped on the kitchen lights, and slipped out of my tie. Shrugging off my sport coat, I tossed it over a tall kitchen table chair and then slipped out of the shoulder holster which held the heavy framed .45 Kimber in it and dropped it on the table top. Unbuttoning the top button of my shirt I turned, opened the big fridge, and pulled out a long neck bottle of German beer I liked and walked out of the kitchen.

I left the kitchen light on and walked through the dining room and entered the semi-darkness of the living room, beer bottle in hand, and flopped into my favorite chair. Outside the storm raged. Rain fell in sheets, hefted around by a brisk breeze. The driving rain kept rattling against the large apartment windows menacingly. Bright slashes of lightning momentarily blazed through the big windows in blinding flashes of raw energy.

I took a swig of the beer and kicked back in the chair casually and stared in front of me. Directly in front of me was a 50 inch LCD monitor for a television set. The TV wasn't on. But, with the kitchen light on behind me, the big black screen in front of me acted like a natural mirror. A mirror that allowed me to see anything in the apartment behind me. That's when I saw him. He momentarily lit up gaudily when a spasm of lightning filled a side window of the apartment, throwing a rectangular beam of light across the room in the process.

There he was. Arturo.

He stood with his back against the wall which divided living room from the dining room. He was dressed normally. But his face was painted. Big splotches of black and green created a nightmare's mirage across the man's face. And his eyes, wide eyes, white and unblinking, staring at the back of my head. In his right hand was one of those bloody jade knives. Bloody—the same one he used in attempting to cut out his sister's heart.

I knew he would be there. Knew it when I was half way up the stairs leading up from the garage floor. The madman may have thought himself a supernatural being, an old Aztec warrior-prince, but running through the rain for most of the night had soaked him to the bone. Thoroughly. He left wet footprints on the wooden stairs. Almost dry by the time I came home. But enough to leave a faint outline in the old wood. Enough to warn me.

Sitting in the chair, my back to him, I took another sip of the beer and then, holding the bottle neck between two fingers, threw my arm across the armrest of the chair and sighed. And then yawned. A second or two later I allowed the empty beer bottle to slowly slide out of my fingers and hit the carpet floor beside the chair. A moment or two ticked by. And then he moved. Moved off the wall and began creeping toward me, his knife hand coming up to his shoulder in preparation for a quick, violent, overhead knife thrust.

His free hand came around the back of the chair and gripped me by the face and yanked my head up violently. At the same time the blade of the obsidian knife came whistling down to drive the blade deep into my throat. But I was ready. The right hand came up and blocked the knife hand. The left hand reached up, grabbed the hand pulling my head up and back, and yanked forward as hard as I could. I twisted around and bent forward from the waist up as well, creating the perfect fulcrum to send Arturo sailing over my head and crashing onto the carpeted floor in front of me.

But he was fast. Very fast. Flying out of my chair I found him standing, bent in a cat-like stance, knife hand up in front of him and ready. He took a vicious swipe at me with the knife. A controlled lunge which forced me to back up. A cruel grin spread across his painted face. The madness in him told him he was in control of the situation. Initially surprised, yes; but in the end he knew he was going to kill me. I could see it clearly written on his face. I saw it in his eyes. He was enjoying the little fight. Enjoying facing someone who actually was resisting him.

I dunno.

Maybe that was it. Maybe it was the smile.

Or maybe the madness in the man's eyes. Or maybe it was his insanity fueled confidence that told him he was going to win in the end. Whatever. But whatever it was, it had suddenly made me immensely angry. This deluded madman was going around killing people as if they were nothing more than his personal trophies. And I was his next trophy. I found myself wanting to hurt him. Hurt him badly. Maybe enough to break a few bones. Maybe even enough to use his own knife against him. Give him a permanent memento to carry around for the rest of his life in some nut house I was going to make damn sure he entered in a fracking straight jacket.

The knife blade came straight at me low and fast. I was faster. One hand snapped forward and gripped the knife hand by his wrist. I lifted the knife hand up and over my head, twisting around ninety degrees in the process. Arturo screamed in pain from having his knife arm half way ripped out of his socket and twisted around as he screamed. My right foot kicked back and caught the madman's left leg just above the knee joint. It folded in half like the blade of a pocket knife. Screaming, he sank to his one good knee howling in pain. But not for long. Bracing myself, I threw a foot up in a kicking blow that caught the madman squarely in the back of the head. His head bounced forward off his chest and up again as if it were a rubber ball just before he pitched forward face first into the floor unconscious.

I turned, stepped up behind the unconscious form, and kicked the ugly looking stone knife across the room before grabbing his knife hand and slapping cold steel for handcuffs around the wrist before reaching for his left hand. I made sure the cuffs were on tight. Stepping back, I backed up to where the television sat. It sat in a wooden cabinet which had both book shelves and wooden drawers in it. Pulling out a drawer I found what I was looking for. Plastic tie downs. Moving back to Arturo I used two of them to bind up his ankles.

I was making damn sure this guy wasn't going to get away again.

I walked into the kitchen to retrieve my cell phone. As I did, the stone blade of the ancient knife came into clear view on the floor beside the dining room table. I stared at it for a moment, and I thought of maybe keeping it for a souvenir. But it was an ugly thing. Ugly and evil. I walked into the kitchen, found my phone, and dialed up the precinct.

Six weeks later, we got a note from the Gomez family. Maria was finally home and recuperating nicely from her traumatic encounter with her brother. And Arturo was in a padded cell in solitary confinement in a hospital in Europe. A hospital noted for its handling of the criminally insane. A hospital with a reputation of its clients entering its enclosed environment, but never leaving.

Unless it was in a coffin. A coffin with their name on it.

7

THE DEAD DON'T COMPLAIN

The stench was enough to make a drug addict with a burnt out septum want to gag. A stench so clawing, so thick, it seemed as if it enveloped you like a rain slick and pressed against your clothes. That's what you get when you find a body that's been dead for about two weeks.

Holding handkerchiefs to our noses, we tried to view the body with a distant, professional gaze. Being homicide detectives, examining dead bodies goes with the territory. No matter how bad they stank or how decomposed they were. But when a body's been dead for two weeks, lying in a bed in an apartment room with the windows closed and locked and no ventilation, even two old dogs like Frank and I thought about transferring to something more mundane like Parks Patrol or Administration.

From what we could tell, the man had been stabbed twice in the heart by a wide, long blade. At one time, the dead man had been in his early forties, going bald, with a body that belonged to an athlete. The two room apartment we found him in was down on Fourth Street. A bad neighborhood filled with drug addicts, prostitutes, and other assorted fauna and flora of the discarded. Just a two room apartment with broken furniture, a battered looking window unit air conditioner in the bedroom, and a big iron bed large enough to sleep maybe three people in it.

Someone had been thorough in searching the dump. The man's clothes were strewn all over the place and ripped to shreds. The large, broken four-drawer chest of drawers had been completely dismantled. Chairs were shredded and pillows ripped to pieces.

Someone was really interested in finding something there. Obviously, something important enough to warrant murder. We stood back and watched the forensics team begin their methodical fugue of the dead. But glancing at my no-necked, red haired Neanderthal wannabe for a partner, I nodded toward the door and silently we made our way out of there.

Frank Morales is the loveable teddy bear kind of guy. If you can imagine a six foot four, three-hundred-pound gorilla with stringy red hair and a chin built out of plate armor as loveable. Actually he is. He's married to an Italian ex-model and has a passel of kids and lives in traditional suburbia. But he's also a cop. A damn good cop. And he's my partner.

"I'm gonna throw away this suit. You'll never wash the stench out of it. Momma's not going to be happy."

I nodded and grinned. Claudia, his wife, would blow a gasket at the thought of throwing away a perfectly good sport coat and slacks only two years off the racks from Walmart. A breathtaking beauty Claudia was. But she was a penny-pinching tight wad as well.

"You'll look good working this case in your underwear and loafers," I quipped, grinning. "Maybe even start a new trend."

"Shut up, pretty boy, and let's go talk to the apartment manager," Frank grunted, a twitch at the corners of his lips—the only kind of grin he had in facial expressions when it came to laughter. "And loan me twenty-five bucks so I can get a decent set of threads."

The grin on my lips widened.

Frank always projected the image of being a poor boy; he claimed he and Claudia only bought clothes either from Walmart or from Goodwill. I knew better. But the red-headed friend of mine and his dazzling wife, I had to admit, were the two most penny-pinching souls I had ever met. They made Ebenezer Scrouge look like a dilettante.

The pretty boy quip he threw at me was an old joke between the two of us. Unfortunately I've got two strikes against me. I'm rich and I have the mug of an old movie star from back in the 30's matinee idol days. Won't mention any names, but the unruly black hair and the thick mustache and dimples are enough to give anyone a jolt—if they know their movie trivia.

The money was an inheritance. It came suddenly and unexpectedly from a grandfather I had, until about three years ago, never met. Before that I—like every other cop I knew—lived from pay check to pay check and felt lucky if I carried a ten dollar bill in my billfold on any given day. But let me tell you, brother, being suddenly rich and with a mug like mine isn't something I'd wish on anyone. You'd think sudden wealth would make me want to leave the cop business and live on a sunny tropical beach somewhere in the Bahamas surrounded by beautiful women. Sorry. Not me. It just so happens I like being a cop.

Listen. If you're a cop and suddenly fall into a shit-pot load of money unexpectedly and from a secretive family member who doesn't like limelight thrown his way, you've got problems. Cops—being cops—are a naturally suspicious lot of cynics. Comes with the territory. So old friends in the department look at me warily. They don't say it to my face but many of them think I'm dirty. I'm on the take.

And yes, to answer the unsaid question, it sticks in my craw.

But those are the crosses I carry. No big deal.

The apartment manager was about five foot four and close to the weight of a Chevy Suburban. He answered his door wearing slacks, chomping on an unlit cigar like it was a loaf of bread, wearing nothing but a t-shirt that did little to hide the thick forest of coarse black hair covering his chest and arms.

"So you gonna clean up that mess up there?" he growled after we showed him our badges. "The sonofabitch is stinking up the whole goddamn building. Someone's gotta kill that stench before it drives out the rest of us."

"We'll remove the body," I said, frowning, pushing my way past him and entering his hovel uninvited. "But sanitizing a rat hole is your kettle of worms. What we want to know is who this guy was. How long has he lived here? When did you see him last alive?"

The fat man's castle looked like it came out of a dumpster. Newspapers were stacked a foot deep beside a worn out looking reclining chair. Beer cans and filled ash trays littered the place. A glance at the kitchen told me the slob must have had a phobia about washing dishes.

I turned back to look at the fat man. He was chewing on his cigar and his cheeks were turning to a kind of purplish crimson. He didn't like me pushing him back and walking into his hive. Tough shit. I didn't like him.

"Listen, before you say something stupid, just give us what we want, and we'll leave. Otherwise we haul your ass downtown and I'll let my partner here introduce himself to you on an intimate basis."

Frank has an interesting trick in his bag of goodies. He can take a can full of beer with his big paw of a hand and squeeze it hard enough to blow the pull-tab off completely. Beer flies out of the can with such force it usually splashes golden rain drops off the ceiling of a room. Sitting on the floor beside the recliner was a six-pack of Budweiser. Not saying a word, Frank bent down, retrieved a can, and demonstrated. It was enough to make the slob reconsider his righteous outrage.

"Called himself John Simmons," he growled, pulling the cigar from his mouth and looking angrily at Frank. "And I just bought that fucking six pack, you ape! Look at the goddamn mess you've made!"

From my slacks I pulled out a money clip and rolled out two twenties and tossed them onto the seat of the recliner.

"That'll cover the damages, friend. Now, next question. How long has John Simmons lived here?"

"Lived here he hasn't. Comes in regularly with a broad or two and spends the weekends. Maybe once or twice during the week as well. But he doesn't live here."

"How long has this been going on?" I asked,

"A couple of years. Maybe a little longer. Pays his rent in cash like clockwork. Never talks to me or to anyone else in the building. Just brings his women in here and screws the hell out of 'em. I get complaints all the time about the noise they make when he brings company. But I don't say a thing. He's about the only person in here who pays his rent on time. I couldn't care less what he did with his women friends as long as I got paid."

"When did you last see him alive?" Frank grunted, tossing the empty beer can onto the man's favorite chair.

"Jesus," the slob grunted, genuinely surprised, as he stuck the stub of his cigar back between his thick lips. "I didn't know apes could talk. But to answer your question, I saw him come in with some bimbo blond about a couple of weeks ago. The woman was a looker. A real class act. Not like the women he usually brought with him. She had money. Lots of money."

"Did they say anything to you?"

"I saw him through my window. They came walking up the sidewalk. The guy owns a fancy car and parks it in a parking building a block over. One of those foreign jobs that costs a lot of money. Red in color with some kind of Italian name I've heard of before."

"Name of the parking building?" Frank asked.

"Claussen's, I think," cigar man said, frowning and lifting a hand to scratch an arm pit. "Over on third. Half way up the block."

We thanked the man for his gracious willingness to help an ongoing investigation and left him standing in the hallway scratching his other armpit absent-mindedly. We walked out of the building and headed for the parking building. A quick walk over to third and we found the parking building and flashed badges into the face of the young black man on duty and told him what we were looking for. A big grin instantly flashed across the kid's face.

"The Lamborghini Contouch. Holy shit! What a gorgeous set of wheels! I get a stiff one just looking at the damn thing. Yeah, it's here. Up on the second deck. Still in one piece. The guy who owns it has paid enough to all of us working here to make sure no one touches it. Big bucks. Here, I'll take you up there and show you."

The kid was more than happy for an excuse to go up and look at the car. Can't say I blamed him. A bright red Lamborghini Contouch is modern Italian sculpture. A Star Wars kinda looking thing on wheels. And it says money as well. About two hundred grand worth.

"Got the keys for it?" I asked, holding out a hand.

"Right here," the kid grinned, reaching over and dropping a

set into my hands. I noticed on the key chain a house key as well.

I opened the driver's side door and carefully looked around. Forensics would be around to give it the detailed once over, so I didn't want to leave stray prints behind. But I did find an insurance card stuffed in a sun screen and used a pair of tweezers to pull it out and look at it.

"Colby Winslow," I said, frowning. "Sounds familiar . . . Colby Winslow."

"He should sound familiar to you, you big oaf," Frank grunted, shaking his head sadly. "He's big in stocks and bonds. Handling a boatload of your money for you. Has an office over on Jones Street."

Grinning, I glanced at the kid staring up at me with big eyes and a surprised face and shrugged. I'll admit it, to be honest, at times, I forget I've got money. Lots of money. I don't handle it myself. When the inheritance came I did some research, found four or five experts in financial planning, and split the inheritance into five equal amounts and let them handle it. Colby Winslow was one of the five.

"Guess you're gonna have to find another money guru, pretty boy."

Smiling, looking at the hunk of Italian steel, I nodded.

"Been here how long?"

"Damn near two weeks," the kid said, white teeth gleaming in the twilight light of the darkly lit parking building. "Way too long for me to guarantee he'll have his set of wheels when he comes back. Already had to run off a couple of bros' who wanted a piece of it."

"Remember the last time you saw him?"

"Sure. When he came in last he came in with that woman of his. *Damn!* Talk about a looker," the kid sighed, hands on his hips, shaking his head in quiet admiration. "Like something out of a movie, mister. Fine. Fine. Fine!"

"Describe her," Frank said, watching the kid and almost smiling.

"Oh shit, legs about a mile long. Wearing a tight blue number that showed every curve she had. And bubba, she had the curves. Long blond hair fell down to her waist. Maybe in her early thirties. Only thing outta place was this big loaf of bread kinda envelope she held tightly under one arm. Like it was money itself. But hell, a woman with legs like that, she could wear a chicken on her head, and I wouldn't give a shit!"

The kid whistled softly through his teeth again and a smile played across his young, handsome face. He was maybe twenty at most. Just a young black kid going to college. I spied the stack of textbooks lying on the desk in the parking booth he occupied when we came up to him.

"He's down here a lot in that car?" I asked.

"Like jelly on toast on the weekends, mister. Always with a different piece of ass. Always."

The kid asked when the guy was coming to pick up his wheels. We told him it wasn't going to happen soon. We left the kid standing beside the Contouch staring at us after we told him a patrol car would be over soon to tape off the parking spot and car. No one was supposed to touch it until then.

Walking back to the flop house, I noticed it was a little past midnight. It was time to go home and get some rest. So we climbed into one of my babies, a dark green with white stripes SS 396 Camaro, lit up the engine, and growled away into the night.

Remember. Rich cop. Collects toys. In this case American made muscle Cars. Yeah, I know. Some collect bottle caps or barbed wire. I collect cars. Go figure.

The next day, we were looking through the desk of Colby Winslow's at his office. In the outer office, two lovely ladies, his secretaries, were crying their hearts out after hearing their boss was dead. Between the two was an elderly man dressed like a conservative banker. He was handing dry tissues to one girl and then to the next as needed. His name was Konrad Bonner and he worked for Winslow as a stock and bonds acquisition expert. The man, in his middle sixties, had been Winslow's first employee. Knew all of the customers the firm serviced. Knew me by my first name.

"Don't worry about your investments, Turner. They're well protected and doing quite well on the market."

"Uh huh," I nodded, frowning as I thought about it. "Who runs this place now that he's dead?"

"Well . . . for the moment, I will, until we can find a buyer for the firm, I suppose."

"A buyer?"

"Turner, this nest is a freakin' cash cow," Frank chided, looking at me and shaking his head. "They invest money—your money, pretty face—and they rake a percentage off each account. Jesus, take a look at his list of clients. Maybe three hundred of'em, and not a one of them worth less than a million. If he rakes in three percent off each client's portfolio . . ."

"Ahumph," the older man growled, lifting a hand politely and clearing his throat, "That would be four and a half percent charge, Detective Morales."

"Damn," my partner grunted, staring at the man in admiration. "That could be millions, Turner. Millions in sheer profit."

"How much would it cost for someone to take over the business?" I asked as I looked the office over.

The ex-banker in his conservative brown suit and wire rimmed glasses mused over the question for a moment or two and then mentioned a number. My eyes narrowed as I turned and stared at the financial genius. A thought crossed my mind. An idea . . .

"Look at this, Turn," Frank said behind me. Twisting around, I saw him lay a big finger on a name written hastily down in a small file book. "Kathryn Valenski. Six p.m.. At Europa's. Dated exactly two weeks ago."

Europa's was a very fancy restaurant on the north side of town. A place where you needed a reservation and a black tie to get in. A place where the food was excellent but about the size of a postage stamp, and it usually cost a couple of C-notes to eat there. Lightly.

"Who is Kathryn Valenski?" I asked, turning my attention back to Bonner. "Another investor?"

"One of our largest," the white haired, bespectacled man nodded, smiling. "I perhaps should clarify that and say her father is one of our largest investors. Although her own portfolio is quite sizeable as well."

"Describe her."

"Long blond hair. Quite tall. In her early thirties. Quite friendly."

"You could describe her as beautiful?" I asked.

"Oh . . . my!"

Yes. The way he said it. The layers of tone in it. Yeah. She was beautiful. Grinning, I nodded and asked Bonner to find her address for me. And as we left the office I handed him one of my cards and told him to give me a call later in the week.

Kathryn Valenski lived in a luxury apartment, top floor, in one of her father's buildings down by the Little Brown River. A doorman dressed like an Italian general opened the glass doors for us as we entered. Entering a cocoon of wealth, the building was as silent as a funeral parlor on a Wednesday afternoon as we rode in silence up the elevator to the nineteenth floor. She met us as the doors opened and we stepped out.

"Did you find them?"

"Find what, Ms. Valenski?" I asked, the first to step out of the elevator.

Let's just say that Kathryn Valenski lived up to her billing. Beautiful. Scratch that. Beautiful simply doesn't come close for a description. Suck the air out of your lungs gorgeous would be a better description.

"The portfolio. The bonds! Did you find them?"

Frank and I watched her face closely. Clearly there was genuine worry in those dark brown eyes of hers. A look of real dread only made her look more breathtakingly gorgeous.

"Let's start from the beginning, Ms. Valenski. I'm Detective Sergeant Turner Hahn and this is my partner Detective Sergeant Frank Morales. We're here investigating the murder of Colby Winslow. We have a few . . ."

"Yes, yes, I know dammit! He's dead. But that doesn't mean anything to me. The one million in unsigned bonds is what I am worried about! If dad finds out they're missing I will be severely pressed to pay him back."

"Your father's bonds?"

"Yes. Part of my inheritance," she said, waving a hand around impatiently before touching her lips, with eyes filling with tears. "Dad told me to take them personally down to Winslow's office and make damn sure they were deposited according to his instructions. So I did and Colby started to . . . well . . ."

"Hit on you," I said bluntly.

"Yes. In only the way he could. He was really a darling, sergeant. Kind. Generous. Handsome in an oafish way. Knew how to make a woman feel wanted."

"So, he invites you to spend a weekend with him in a sleaze hole down on Fourth Street?" I said, sounding distinctly suspicious, as my eyes played across her face. "I betcha your father has a Learjet. Why not a weekend in Las Vegas instead?"

"Las Vegas is so passé," she answered, her voice filled with discord. "Been there a thousand times."

"But a run-down shanty flop house on Fourth street was something new to you," Frank grunted sarcastically.

She hesitated, nodded, biting on a perfectly manicured fingernail with eyes tearing again.

"Oh, I know I sound horrible! More concerned about dad's money than about poor Colby getting murdered by that . . . by that . . . woman! But he convinced me to go with him into that part of town and walk on the fringes of darkness. To taste danger and crime at an intimate level. I . . . I . . . god help me! I found myself hypnotized by his words. I agreed. We left his office immediately and drove down in his car. Left so fast we forgot to deposit the bonds in his safe. He laughed, said carrying such a large bundle of wealth around like it was a grocery sack would make the experience more titillating!"

"What happened next?"

"Drink?" she asked, looking intently into both of our faces before turning and entering her apartment, talking over her shoulder. "I need a drink. A very stiff one. Scotch maybe. Or Jim Beam."

She had a stiff drink. Big glass. Two cubes of ice. Half full. Drank it down like a submariner straight off a six month stint at sea. She was beautiful. Rich. Bored. And a well-kept lush. Trouble quadrupled. I watched and said nothing until she drained the fuel tank.

"You were saying?"

"Ah, the woman. Well, let me see," she sighed, reaching up with a hand to pull on one strand of hair which had slipped across the front of her shoulder. "We got there late. Maybe around eight or nine that night. We fooled around a little and then I got up and went to the bathroom. I was in there only a few moments and then I hear this angry pounding on the apartment door and a woman screaming furiously! I slip my clothes back on and open the bathroom door just enough to see what's going on. My god! What anger she had! Absolutely furious and waving this big knife around like a madwoman!"

She poured another glass of booze. This time topping the glass and stirring the ice around with a finger as she stared at the dark liquid and relived the night two weeks earlier.

"What happened, Ms. Valenski?"

"Huh? Oh. She came in screaming and waving that knife around and demanding to know where this bitch was he was with that night. Wanted to know where I was, sergeant. Me! Said she was going to kill us both. I got so frightened I . . . I don't mind admitting it. I almost fainted with terror."

"Winslow tried to stop her and that's when she knifed him," Frank pitched in behind me. But the tone in his voice told me he wasn't buying it. Any of it.

"No. Just the opposite, dammit. He laughs. Colby just laughed at her. She's dancing all around him waving this big fucking knife around like some witchdoctor and he just turns with her and laughs at her like it was some kind of big joke! It was the most outrageous. . . most erotic . . . sight I had ever seen!"

"She doesn't kill him," I put in, priming the pump again.

"No! Not then. Not at that moment. Instead a hand flashes out and he slaps the knife from the woman's hand. He grabs her and crushes her to his chest and buries' his lips onto hers. And that's when I left detectives. He turned her away from the bathroom door and motioned me to leave and leave fast. I left. Left as fast as I could."

"Left forgetting the portfolio and the bonds behind," I said.

"Oh my god, yes! Ran for my life, dammit. Ran like a frightened little girl."

"But you came back," Frank grunted behind me. "And found?"

Tears rolled down her perfectly formed cheeks as she played with fingernails across her lips and nodded. God. She was good. A rich, bored, beautiful lush. But a great actress as well. Hollywood missed out in not throwing her up on a silver screen. She was that good.

"Came back. Found Colby dead. Blood all over him and that bloody knife lying on the floor beside the bed. I took the knife and I . . . I went crazy looking for the bonds. I must have torn the place to pieces looking for them. But they were gone. Gone."

"You touched the knife, leaving your fingerprints on it?" I asked.

She nodded, watery eyes filled with fear.

"But you didn't kill Colby Winslow."

She nodded again—meaning she didn't kill Colby Winslow.

"This woman who came in with the knife, can you describe her?" Frank asked.

Tall. Thin. Flat. About thirty. Kinda cute in a tomboyish way. An athlete. Raven black hair. She remembered seeing her several times over the years in Colby's office. She was sure the tomboy was another investor.

"Okay, we'll find her," I said, nodding and turning to leave. "But just to let you know, Ms. Valenski. Right now your number one on our suspect list. If I were you I'd call daddy up and get him to find you a good lawyer. A team of good lawyers."

On the way down in the silence of the elevator I half turned and asked.

"Believe her?"

There was a grunt. Maybe more like a hippo snorting.

"Maybe. Let's see if we can find the knife-wielding chick."

We did. It took a few phone calls. A little footwork. Cop work is like that. Ask questions. Make some phone calls. Slide miles of leather across hard pavement. Ask more questions. A lot more questions. Repeat the process.

Her name was Gail. Gail Oppenheimer. Widow of a man who became wealthy creating a string of gym/martial arts palaces across four states. She still taught classes herself. Her specialty was fencing. Cold steel. Long blades.

Violet colored eyes watched us with a quiet resignation registered in them. She saw us enter her place and knew instantly who we were. Frank and I both dress in comfortable slacks, sport coats, comfortable shoes. We wear shades. Either we're classy thugs working for some mobster, or we're cops. She chose correctly.

"You're here to arrest me, aren't you detectives?" she whispered, looking up at me as she sat behind a wide desk in her office.

"Maybe," I nodded but not sounding optimistic. "Depends on what you say. Depends on what the evidence tells us. But you know why we're here."

She nodded, ran a calloused, fighter's hand across her face and used a finger to wipe a tear out of the corner of her eye.

"I have a temper, detective. One that can sometimes get out of hand. But that doesn't mean I killed Colby. I couldn't kill him. I loved him too much."

"Just start from the beginning and tell us what happened that night," I said.

The two of us stood in front of her desk while I looked the office over. She had an office with two large plate glass windows, which looked out into the main part of the dojo. As I looked, two men wearing the black pajamas of karate instructors stood side by side and watched us with silent interest. Behind her on the walls were row after row of trophies of various sizes. And swords. Several different lengths of fencing foils, rapiers, knives, and daggers.

This woman was seriously in love with cold steel.

"I saw Colby leave with Kathryn Valenski that night. Saw them get into Colby's car. I knew where they were going. To his love nest. To screw her. After he had promised me the night before we would go down there for the weekend. I blew up. I went crazy. Followed them down there. Pounded on the door, wanting to catch them in bed."

"To kill them," Frank grunted.

"I know I must have screamed something like that at him. But no. I couldn't kill Colby. Love is a terrible mistress, gentlemen. I've known his infidelities. I know he didn't love me. Sex addicts usually don't love anyone but themselves. But I loved him. Loved him terribly."

"But you did come at him with a knife. A very big knife," I put in.

"Just to scare him. Just to frighten him. Just to show him how much he meant to me!"

"And it worked?"

"Ha!" came the barking reply. "Colby knew me too well. He just laughed at me. Just laughed and took the knife out of my hands and threw it to one side. And then he grabbed me and took me into the bedroom. We made love that night. Several times. All weekend. Sunday afternoon I had to leave him lying in bed asleep. I had a major tournament to go to and I had to leave."

"He was alive when you left him?" I asked.

"Yes. Alive and sleeping like a baby."

"What about the portfolio?"

"What portfolio?" she asked as curiosity lit up her face.

"You mean that big brown bundle Kathryn carried with her? Oh. That. I dunno. I saw it lying on the coffee table in front of the divan when I came in. Thought nothing of it. As far as I know it was still on the coffee table when I left."

One of the two male instructors walked away as several students entered the dojo. The other, a tall man with big hands and a bushy mane, remained standing on a mat and watched us intently. He looked concerned. He kept reaching up and rubbing his lips in a fitful gesture of someone really nervous about something. A gesture both Frank and I were quite used to seeing.

"When did you go back to the apartment?" I asked, returning my attention back to the woman.

"I didn't. The tournament went on all afternoon and late into the night. When it was over, I drove back to my place and went to bed."

"And that's the last time you saw Colby alive?" Frank asked behind me,

"The last time," she nodded.

"When we came in here you knew why we were here. Knew who we were," I began, my voice hard. "We're homicide detectives. You knew he was dead. How?"

She shrugged with a smile of infinite sadness on her boyish lips.

"I just knew. I've been calling his office, his apartment, just about every number I know trying to find him. Every day for two weeks. And then last night, for some odd reason, I drove down to the parking garage where he always parked his Lamborghini and saw it still in the same slot he had parked it in two weeks ago. That's when I began to fear the worst. You two coming into the dojo confirmed it."

I nodded and glanced out the window. The big man with

the shabby mop of hair was gone. Frowning, I glanced at Frank and then looked back at Gail Oppenheimer.

"Did anyone else know you loved Colby Winslow? Anybody here in the dojo, for instance?"

She nodded with a cloud of questioning filling her eyes.

"It's no secret. The staff and I are quite close. We share our woeful tales of our love lives almost daily here. Both Doug and Marlin—my instructors—knew how I felt for him. Why do you ask?"

"If you didn't kill Colby Winslow and Kathryn Valenski didn't kill Colby Winslow, who did? Who else had a motive to stab a man to death and steal a million dollars in bonds?'

"A million dollars . . . in bonds! Oh, my god! Marlin!"

"Marlin? Big man, shaggy mop of hair, one of your instructors?" Frank asked, frowning.

"He's been moping around in the dojo for a week or two now. But he bought himself a brand new car. Said he paid cash for it. Said he'd won some cash on a roulette table in a casino in Kansas City. My god. Marlin!"

"What about Marlin?" Frank asked irritably.

"Oh . . . Marlin has had a crush on me since the day I hired him. He thinks he's in love with me. But I always thought it was just an infatuation. Still, he always was forceful in his efforts to dissuade me from getting involved with Colby. Very heatedly so sometimes."

"Where does Marlin live, Ms. Oppenheimer?"

She quickly wrote it down and handed us the paper. Without another word, we left and climbed into the Camaro SS and left. About the time I pulled away from the curb, the cell phone buzzed loudly inside my sport coat.

"Turn, this is Joe down at the morgue. Thought you should know. The dead guy? Someone popped him in the jaw with a big hand and big ring. Broke the jaw. Didn't see the bruising at the crime scene because the body was too decomposed. But a closer look at it down here and it's obvious as hell. I'm pretty sure it was a man who killed your dead guy."

Joe was Joe Weiser, a smart-assed, gum-chewing kid for a forensics expert who worked with the coroner down at the morgue. Kid or not, Joe was damn good at his job. If he said he thought a big man with big hands was our probable killer that's all I needed to know. It fit.

Fit indeed.

We found Marlin at his apartment hurriedly throwing clothes into a suitcase. When we walked in, he glanced at a .357 magnum lying on the bed beside the suitcase. But, glancing at us and seeing us shaking our heads and reaching for our own iron, he decided a sudden invitation to lie on a morgue slab himself was not the way he wanted to go down.

Let me tell you, friend. Money will get you in trouble. Money and beautiful women will kill you. And oh yeah. The old ex-banker and I got together. Seems like now I am a part-owner in a thriving investment company.

8

DISILLUSIONED

He opened the door and stepped into the Spartan furnished interrogation room, nodding to his partner silently. His partner was a massive hulk of a creature with short, carrot colored red hair. Hair which absolutely revolted at the thought of being combed. The red haired giant grimaced, frowned, and tilted his head toward the man sitting across from him.

He eyed the suspect, lifting an eyebrow curiously.

Mister Average American.

Roughly five foot ten. Brown hair. Brown eyes. Dressed in faded, comfortable looking, old, blue jeans and an off white pullover for a shirt. Like him, the guy needed a shave. There were bags underneath his eyes from lack of sleep and deep emotional trauma. Trauma reflected in the whites of his eyes.

"This is Frank Gorman, Turner. Husband to the deceased. Frank walked into the precinct house about a half hour ago and surrendered himself. He admits killing his wife. Says he did it in a fit of rage. Just lost it after a heated argument. He doesn't remember killing her. Just that he killed her."

Turner Hahn, his partner in homicide, nodded, his eyes not leaving the suspect's face as his red-headed partner filled in the pertinent details. The silence of the cramped interrogation room contained a harsh, brittle feeling of immense remorse. Frank Gorman looked guilty. The man's eyes never wavered from staring at the dark level of black fluid of what some people might euphemistically call coffee in his cup. Both Turner and Frank saw the little droplets of dark red smudges splattered across the right side of his shirt. They had glimpsed something dark and semi dried under the man's fingernails on his right hand. Undoubtedly blood. They were sure forensics would probably confirm it was his wife's blood. Conclusively.

Yes. Frank Gorman had all the looks of a guilty man.

Visual evidence alone was enough to convince any jury he killed his wife. Patrol officers at the murder scene already confirmed the man's story that he and his wife had been arguing loudly for several hours. Arguing loud enough for the neighbors on both sides of the deceased's house to hear plainly. Confirming, of course, the man's statement.

But . . .

Turner slid his dark gray-blue eyes away from the suspect and looked at his partner's ugly mug and almost smiled. Frank Morales . . . his partner . . . had a face as stoic and unreadable as a block of dark granite. Unreadable to just about anyone who knew his partner. But not to him. To him, Frank was like an open book waiting to be read. This Frank, *his* Frank, had a look on him he was all too familiar with.

Frank Morales, his partner, felt uneasy about the man's confession. Didn't necessarily mean the guy was innocent. But maybe not guilty either. But there was something—a little spark of doubt, a little flicker of curiosity—which made Frank uneasy. A wiry grin spread across his thin lips. He knew his partner like he knew every screw and spring and polished blue steeled part of the .45 caliber Kimber riding in its holster underneath his left armpit. Frank had an IQ somewhere north, far north, of 185. No question, the giant was a freaking genius. It was common knowledge in the precinct house that Frank knew everything. Ask him an intelligent question which required a thinking answer, and you got an immediate, instant, response. So far, in the last fifteen years, no one had stumped the red-headed Godzilla.

Which was axiomatic. *If* Frank Morales doubted Frank Gorman's confession, it meant something was there he wasn't seeing. Which meant he had to do some digging for himself.

"Doctor Gorman, I'm Detective Turner Hahn, Detective Morales' partner. Mind if I sit down and ask you a few questions?"

Silence.

Turner Hahn pulled a chair up from the corner of the room and sat down beside his partner. It was an interesting pairing. Height wise, Turner was as tall as Frank. Both stood around six foot four, but Frank weighed around three hundred pounds of mostly solid muscle and thick gristle, while Turner moved the scales a little over two hundred and fifty five of muscle and lankiness. Together, the two made for one excellent team of homicide detectives.

"In your confession, you said you and your wife were arguing. Can you tell us what the argument was about?"

"We were arguing about money. Always about money."

"How much money?" Frank asked, his voice the rumble of a truck load of gravel over a speed bump. "A couple of hundred? A couple of thousand? More?"

"Uh . . . well . . . more like half a million. We needed to find a half million dollars before the end of next month. I didn't think we could raise it. I wanted to sell the practice. Get it off our hands. Maybe start over. But Cherri wouldn't hear of it.

Said she had spent too many years building the practice up. Starting over was not an option."

"You and your wife worked together?" Turner asked.

It took a second or two, but it finally happened. The man moved. Barely nodding his head as he stared down at his coffee cup despondently.

"What kind of practice is this?" Frank asked.

"We are . . . were . . . practicing psychologists. Both of us have our PhD's in Psychology. We've been working on our practice for more than five years now. That's . . . uh . . . why we are in so much debt. Last year we moved into a brand new building built to our specifications. We thought we were properly funded. But we were wrong. One of our financiers pulled out of the project, dumping the half million debt into our laps unexpectedly."

Turner grunted, half grinned, and nodded. He saw the conundrum his partner was mentally wrestling with. The guy walks into the precinct house . . . a highly intelligent, extremely articulate professional . . . and confesses killing his wife . . . yet says he doesn't remember doing it.

Odd.

"Doctor Gorman," Turner began, the grin disappearing from his lips. "Lead us into this tiff you and your wife were in and all the way up to where you blacked out. Tell us everything you remember."

Tears welled up in the man's eyes and began sliding down his cheeks in narrow, meandering rivulets. Whatever color was left in his cheeks drained. His hands began to shake visibly as he continued to hold onto the coffee cup.

The argument started in a restaurant he, his wife, and his step son were dining at earlier in the evening. Mark, his step son, was very angry at his mother. She had promised to help him buy a car so he could go back to college driving something more reliable. But this five hundred thousand was putting the brakes on that promise. Every dime was going in trying to pay off the debt. Mark was furious and demanded to know why he had to suffer all the time whenever something between the two shrinks came up.

That last comment from Mark sent his wife down the path of accusing him, Frank Gorham, of being too lax in checking the backgrounds of his financiers. It was *his* fault they all were in the financial dumps they were in. Of course he became angry at being portrayed as the bad guy. Again. Whenever a financial crisis popped up which affected the family he was always accused of being the instigator. So the argument between his wife and her son engulfed the entire family and continued to escalate through the diner and all the way back to their home.

Mark left the house in a fit of rage, screaming that both he and his mother were not only outright quacks, but quacks who did not even rise to the level of witch doctors. They were nothing more than brazen liars and thieves. When Mark slammed the door behind him, Cherri lost it. She went ballistic. Started screaming at Frank. Throwing pots and pans—anything she could grab off the kitchen counter tops—screaming at the top of her lungs that she wanted a divorce and wanted to destroy his sorry lying ass for deceiving her.

The doctor said he remembered batting the thrown objects away from him, but something caught him above his right eyebrow. Something heavy. He remembered staggering back and half falling onto a kitchen counter top. Pushing himself upright again, he remembered seeing the wooden block filled with sharp carving knives sitting on the cabinet right beside his hands. After that . . .

He remembered waking up and staring up at the kitchen's ceiling fan. He remembered noting the incredible sound of absolute silence which filled the house deafeningly. He remembered rolling over onto a shoulder and seeing his wife lying right beside him. Blood everywhere. That's when he knew—knew he had killed his wife. He climbed to his feet, making sure not to disturb anything in the kitchen, and went down to the garage. From there he drove straight over to the precinct house and turned himself in.

The confession was a mere whisper coming from the man's lips. Cold, impersonal, almost hypnotic in its delivery. He would pause occasionally, wipe a stream of tears from his cheeks with the back of a hand, and continue his story. But the hand always returned to its original grip on the coffee cup. As he spoke, both Frank and Turner could mentally see the visuals the quiet confessor described.

They weren't pretty. But they were all too familiar.

Turner nodded, got up, and walked to the door.

"That's all of our questions for now, Dr. Gorman. You'll return to the holding cell, and later on, you'll be transported downtown to the jail where you'll be formally processed."

A burly looking police officer filled the doorway and waited for the psychologist to come to his feet.

We watched the shrink being escorted down a hall and disappear around a corner. Frank grunted in interest and looked at Turner.

"A smart guy walks into a police station and confesses to a murder even he really doesn't know he committed. Why?"

"Maybe he's so smart he thinks a good acting job will convince us he's innocent."

"Maybe he is innocent," returned the red-headed mass of muscle and bone. "Maybe he's taking the fall to protect someone."

"Maybe like . . . the stepson?"

"Maybe. Maybe someone else we haven't met yet."

"Maybe. But you really don't think the shrink did it?"

"No, I don't."

"Maybe, my big, ugly red-headed stepchild of a buddy, you oughta tell me why *you* think he's innocent."

The Maybe Game. A quirky word game the two had come up with a few years back to quickly bounce ideas back and forth to each other, and at the same time, to take the tension out of the air with a little mirth in the process.

Frank lifted his red-bearded, cement block of a head up and trained his amazingly small, brown eyes onto the image of his friend standing beside him in the hallway. Running a hand uselessly through his stringy, red hair to get it momentarily off his forehead, the massive creature almost grinned.

"Maybe I don't really know. Call it a hunch. A hint. A tremulous intuitive afterthought."

Mischief sparkled in Turner's eyes and his lingering grin widened. A kid's smirk of pure smart-assery.

"A *tremulous* intuitive afterthought? That's almost poetic. Is it something like feminine intuition?"

"Maybe."

"Maybe," Turner echoed. "Poetic or feminine?"

Frank didn't answer. Just shrugged his massive shoulders in silence.

Turner grinned wider, punched his partner's shoulder playfully, and started moving.

"Well, whatever it is, my *very* big friend and partner, let's go earn our money and ask some questions. And by the way, pull your skirt down. Your slip is showing."

Look it up in the dictionary. Police Work is defined as: *A Mobius Loop. (1) The constant occurrence of asking the same questions over and over without let up. (2) The continuance of a cycle of interviewing the same witnesses, bystanders, and possible suspects until a new name is added to the list of witnesses, bystanders, and possible suspects.* (3) *Sheer. Mind-numbing. Boredom.*

It's the third definition that is important. It's the one that separates the wannabe cops from the real ones. In any mindless operation, the one who can spot the anomaly in the day-to-day routine is the one who succeeds. The one who gets promoted from patrolman to detective. The detective, or detective team, who has the highest conviction rates.

They found a few anomalies worth investigating.

The first anomaly was they couldn't find Gorman's stepson, Mark. He was gone. Not at home. Not in any of the city's three hospitals. In no one's morgue. Not crashing at some buddy's apartment. He was just . . . *gone.*

The search did find Mark's car parked in a parking lot off Davidson Street. A big lot pushed up against a giant chain bookstore. He drove a typical college kid set of wheels; a relatively new Chevy Camaro. Oddly, Mark's keys were still in the ignition. The driver's side window was down four or five inches. The cramped back seat of the car was loaded down with a jumbled mass of clothes and college textbooks hurriedly thrown back there as if Mark was in a rush to leave. But there was no Mark.

The second anomaly was Cherri Gorman's newly amended will. She didn't leave a penny to either Frank or her son. Not one red cent.

The two drove back to the precinct house and sat their only suspect down in the same plain, wooden chair in the same barren interrogation room as before. But this time, Frank sat in the chair across from Gorman, and Turner's large frame leaned against the wall behind his partner and remained silent.

"Dr. Gorman, why did your wife suddenly change her will? And why did she erase you and your stepson from it?"

"I . . . uh . . ." he cleared his throat softly as he squirmed a little in his seat, "don't really know. She . . . she just informed Mark and I the other night when we dined out about it. We were . . . were . . . equally . . . astonished to hear it."

Gorman sat in the chair, hands clasped together on top of the table, eyes cast downward and staring at his hands. His complexion was very pale.

Turner leaned against the one-way glass mirror behind him, folded his arms across his chest, and eyed the suspect closely. Yet his mind was shouting at him, formulating "what if's?" and playing them across his consciousness like a tape recorder. What were the probabilities in cracking this case? Who was the real victim here? Was the good doctor sitting at the table a consummate liar? Or maybe, just maybe . . . *The perfect crime, the perfect crime,* a small voice repeated over and over, like a pair of incessant castanets. Nevertheless, he kept silent as Frank rumbled up another volcanic sounding verbalization which, quite naturally, made the room quiver and shake ever so minutely at the sub atomic level.

"Your wife changed her will a little over a week ago. Suddenly and without warning. Are you sure you have no idea what was in her mind to do this?"

Gorman's eyes flickered, flickered upward and toward Frank's massive form sitting across from him. His hand moved, rolled once in a revolving ball of flesh and then stopped. He coughed gently as his eyes settled on Frank's granite shaped face.

"I'm not sure. I really don't know . . . but . . . but a week before Cherri saw her lawyer, I know she had a long conversation on the phone with her ex-husband. Apparently Wilson . . . Cherri's ex . . . moved back to town. He called to inform Cherri he was back and wanted to touch . . . touch base with her. And, I guess, ask if it was possible to see Mark again."

"Your wife had been married before? How long ago?"

"Before . . . before I met her in graduate school. Mark was just a baby then. Maybe a year old. Maybe two. I don't remember."

"Why did they split up, Dr. Gorman? Why this long period of silence between the two?"

"Uh . . . uh . . . as I understand it, Wil . . . Wilson has been in prison all this time. He served out his term and was released about . . . about a month ago. Or, at least, that's what Cherri told me the other night."

Frank sat back in his chair and folded arms across his chest before twisting his head around to glance at Turner. Turner, for his part, frowned as he glanced at his partner and silently mouthed the question, *"Where's Mark?"* Frank nodded and twisted back around to look at Gorman.

"Doctor Gorman, we're trying to find Mark, but so far, we haven't had any luck. We found his car in a big lot over on Davidson Street. You have any idea where we might find him?"

"Davidson Street? By a large bookstore? Ah. I . . . uh . . . believe his girlfriend lives across the street. She rents a small efficiency apartment above a coffee shop. She works part time in the bookstore while she goes to school here in town. You . . . you might find him there."

"What's her name?"

"Cassandra, I think. That's all Mark called her. Just Cassandra."

Frank Gorman's body seemed to deflate before their eyes and his color worsened. Both detectives knew there would be no more information coming out of the doctor's mouth today. Frank stood up and knocked gently on the interrogation room's only door. When the door closed behind the departing two, Frank turned to face Turner.

"Need to find out about his wife's first husband. Especially the part about being in prison for so long."

Turner nodded in silence in agreement. Frank, reading Turner's face, made a scowling face.

"Okay, Detective Sergeant Hahn . . . spill it. What's percolating in the pea pod sized brain of yours?"

Turner smiled.

"We've worked some tough cases haven't we, buddy?"

Frank nodded.

"Cases we thought for a while we weren't gonna crack open. Cases each of us thought, in the back of our minds, was going to turn out to be that one mythical creature. That perfect crime."

"You think this is the one? You think that guy cooked up a murder and planned it so well he's gonna get away with it?"

Turner grinned, nodded.

Frank scowled again.

"Okay, buddy. Tell me this. How much you wanna bet? How much you got on you right now?"

Turner's sardonic grin widened. Frank knew exactly what his partner was worth. He kept no secrets from his partner.

"The last time I checked the balance on my credit card, somewhere between maybe twenty . . . twenty-five million."

"Asshole," Frank grunted, reaching back and pulling out his billfold and grabbing the only greenback he had in it. "I got five dollars says you're wrong. Dead wrong. Five bucks says Frank Gorman is innocent and his wife's ex-husband is our killer. Wanna bet?"

Turner, still grinning, nodded his head and said, "Sure."

Frank took the lead. Walking out of the interrogation room, Turner followed the hulking giant in front of him as they exited the precinct house and climbed into Turner's car.

"Where to?" the smiling, ersatz matinee movie idol asked.

"Davidson Street . . . and step on it, James."

Twenty minutes later, the two went thumping up a set of

stairs and to the second floor above the coffee shop and down a short hall to Apartment No. 4. They came to a halt a few feet from the door. In front of Apartment 4 stood a Guatemalan woman and a short, Chinese man, their faces filled with concern. Behind them, the apartment doors of two and three were partially open.

"You smell that?" the woman said, turning and looking at Turner and Frank. "I know that smell. It's just like the smell in Guatemala. The smell of death."

Both detectives smelled it. It was unmistakable.

Walking into the apartment, they found the source of the odor.

Turner, face set in an unreadable mask, turned half way and eyed the two.

"Can either of you two identify this woman. Is this Cassandra?"

The two glanced at each other, the man shrugged and the woman nodded, before turning back to look at Turner.

"Noooo . . . we're pretty sure that's not Cassandra, detective. I think that's her sister, Kelly. Cassandra's been gone for the last week. Went back to visit her parents. She told me she'd be gone exactly one week. It's been one week. I've been expecting her to show up sometime today."

Turner glanced at Frank. Frank reached inside his sport coat and pulled out his cellphone and thumbed in a number quickly.

The two cleared out of the apartment when the mob of technical people showed up. Descending the stairs, they stepped outside into the late afternoon sun and were immediately hit with the powerful aroma of strong coffee rolling out of the small coffee shop. There were a few empty tables on the sidewalk in front of the store, along with about six other tables filled with college students and young professionals chatting away casually and sipping on lattes. A young college kid with a fresh white apron came out as Turner and Frank sat down to take their order. Just as the kid disappeared into the dark confines of the coffee shop, a cab slid to a halt in front of a jumbled row of sidewalk tables. The driver got out, walked back to the rear of the car, popped open the car's trunk and begin pulling out heavy looking suitcases. The back door of the taxi opened as well and out stepped the elusive Cassandra.

She looked almost exactly like the sister upstairs. Cassandra, however, had the look of a weary traveler. Her long brown hair was in serious need of brushing. Her slacks and blouse looked as if she had slept in them. She had the exhausted, frustrated look every traveler has after dealing with airline clerks and overcrowded airplanes.

It was Frank who got up from the table and approached the young girl, his gold detective badge in his hand at the ready. Turner watched his partner quietly inform Cassandra of the bad news. As expected, the news of her sister's murder and her boyfriend's disappearance destroyed her. She collapsed into Frank's arms.

Turner stood up, grabbed an empty chair from one of the tables, and sat it down between them just as Frank gently deposited Cassandra into it. Turning, he flashed his gold badge to the onlookers, told them that this was delicate police business, and asked them to take their coffee and their conversations into the coffee shop and give them a little room.

Turner and Frank remained silent and waited for the young woman to regain her composure. Tears flowed freely down her cheeks. Her body shivered several times underneath the sidewalk cafe's canopy from the intense emotion sweeping through her. Eventually, her tears began to subside.

"I know this may be impossible to accomplish right now, Cassandra. But we need to find Mark. Your boyfriend," Frank began, sounding amazingly gentle and empathic for a guy that would make a mountain gorilla look anemic.

"Mark? Did he . . . did he kill my sister?"

Her eyes filled with tears, and it looked as if she was about to have another emotional upheaval, but she fought the wave of despair off and looked at Frank with an intense, pleading look on her lovely face.

"No, no. Nothing like that. But we are concerned for Mark's safety. I have to tell you that your sister is not the only one who has been murdered, Cassandra. Mark's mother was murdered as well."

"Oh . . . my god! Who . . . who killed her?"

"Mark's step-father has confessed to murdering his wife. He claims he doesn't remember a thing about it. But he's sure it must have been him."

"Oh, it was him, all right. It was that sonofabitch who killed her! No doubt about that!"

Traumatic pain had been replaced. Replaced in the beating of a living heart with a fiery flash of intense anger. It was a complete turnaround of emotions.

"Mark told me everything. Everything about that bastard!"

"What did Mark tell you?" Frank echoed.

"Mark's step-father has been stealing money from his mother for the last year or more. Somehow he figured out a way to take control of the finance company, which is supposedly giving them the money to build the building for their expanded practice. So far he's stolen almost a million dollars from them. A million dollars!"

"How did Mark discover this?" Turner asked.

"His father told him. John Wilson. Mark's father got out a prison about a month ago and called Mark to tell him he wanted to see him. Said it was really important. He told Mark that, while in prison, he met inmates who knew his step-father, Dr. Gorman. Knew him *before* he became a psychologist."

"Mark believed his father?" Turner said.

"Absolutely!" Cassandra nodded, her eyes filling with tears. "Mark said he did some digging on his own. Said he knew some friends who knew some of his step-dad's patients in the clinic. Said each one of them, after seeing Dr. Gorman, had almost been financially ruined soon afterwards. He did some more digging and found out, with his father's help, that Dr. Gorman somehow had manipulated the loan company who held the note on the new building. Every dime the Gorman's paid on the building's new construction was actually going into his step dad's pocket!"

"What was Mark going to do with this news, Cassandra?" Frank asked, a murderous scowl falling across the red-haired man's face.

"Mark was going to confront his step-father directly. Said he and his mother and Dr. Gorman were scheduled to go out to a restaurant in a few days to eat. He said that would give him time to collect all the evidence he needed to convince his mother he was telling her the truth.

"I . . . I told him that was foolish. Maybe he ought to go to the police first. Expose his step-father to people who knew how to handle something like this. But Mark was adamant. Said he hated his step-father. Said he needed to look him directly in his eyes and call him a fraud and a blackmailer to his face. I couldn't stop him. I had to catch a plane and go see my parents. Everything was all arranged. I . . . I should have stayed here and done something to protect Mark and his mother."

Cassandra melted into a spasm of tears and remorse. The two giants for detectives sat patiently and waited for the emotional release of the young girl to eventually drain away.

After that, the two put her in a squad car, took her to a safe house, and deposited her there.

In silence, the two drove back to the precinct and asked for the return of Dr. Gorman to the interrogation room.

When Turner and Frank entered the room, they found two people waiting for them. Sitting in the same chair he sat in the last time they had interviewed him was Dr. Frank Gorman. He looked almost exactly like the last time. Quiet, timid. Drained of any facial expression.

Sitting beside Gorman was a man both detectives knew all too well. James Concannon. Defense attorney. He sat with a smirk on his lips beside his client, the top of his bald head shining underneath the room's lights.

"My client has asked me to represent him in this, gentlemen. He claims extenuating circumstances forced him to confess to the crime committed against his wife. I believe we can build a case which proves my client is innocent. At least, that is our intent."

Frank grunted something under his breath as he eyed his partner and then tilted his head toward the table the two sat at. Turner, nodding, pulled the chair directly across from the two and sat down.

"Fine, fine. To ever man his proper due. But I must warn you, I have a partner who is very upset with your client, counselor."

Concanon, knowing Frank all too well, lifted eyes and gazed at the hulking mass of bone and flesh behind Turner and frowned.

"Why is he upset?"

"He lost a bet," Turner answered, a smile of boyish delight painted on his face. "You know Frank. He's never wrong on just about everything there is to know. As far as I know, he's been wrong on only two occasions. Each one revolving around a homicide case. Each one a bet he made with me."

"What was the bet?" the defense attorney asked hesitantly.

"Frank believed your client. Thought he was innocent. I didn't."

Frank Gorman's eyelids fluttered. For a second, Turner thought the quiet man was going to lift them up and glance at Frank. But they didn't move.

Just as Concannon was about to say something, someone rapped softly twice on the interrogation room's door. Frank came off the wall, walked over to the door, opened it, grunted a "thanks" and then closed the door softly in front of him. In his left hand were two long objects. Baseball bats. Two wooden bats. Thick and polished and glistening in the soft lighting of the room. Frank hefted them up in front of him and almost smiled as he walked back to the wall behind his partner and casually sat one of the bats against the wall beside him. The red-headed giant gripped the other with both of his massive hands and grunted in pleasure.

"Say, what the hell is going on here? Are you trying to intimidate me and my client, Detective Hahn? Here? In this room?"

"Oh no, no, no . . . counselor. We would never do that," Turner, that impish smirk on his lips widening, answered. "We know better. Besides, this interview is being taped. We'll certainly give you a copy of it as evidence if you want one. No . . . the bats are here to keep Frank occupied while we talk. Like I said, my partner is upset. He actually took in your client's cockamamie story hook, line, and sinker. So he needs to channel is frustration out in a non-violent manner. So to speak."

"So . . ." began the bespectacled lawyer hesitantly, glancing at Turner in front of him and then quickly looking over Turner's right shoulder and back at the red-headed giant behind him. "What is he going to do with them?"

The answer came quickly enough, and loudly, like the unexpected explosion of a powerful revolver going off in a very tiny room.

CRACK!

Frank snapped the major league baseball bat made of polished maple in half. He had gripped it with both hands and just jerked his hands in one short, powerful roll of the wrists. The noise was so loud that both Concannon and his client visibly flinched in their chairs.

"Jesus, detective! You . . . you . . . don't call this a form of intimidation!? What the hell are you trying to do here? Scare us? Well . . . let me tell you . . . you've certainly scared me!"

Turner chuckled. Frank tossed the two pieces of wood casually into the empty metal trash can in the corner of the room.

"Your client lied to us, counselor. Oh, he confessed to murdering his wife. But only in a way that would immediately create doubt in any juror's mind. Claiming amnesia? Yet forthright enough to confess to a murder he may not have done? A brilliant performance, Dr. Gorman. Brilliant. You were betting that, in the end, a jury of your peers would give you the benefit of doubt and let you off the hook. But you made one, if not two, fatal mistakes, doctor. Mistakes that are going to send you to prison for the rest of your life."

"What mistakes?" Gorman's counselor growled, narrowing eyes suspiciously.

"We're not charging your client with just the murder of his wife, counselor. We're bringing multiple charges of murder against him. We believe your client not only murdered his wife, but he also killed his step-son, along with a man by the name of John Wilson . . . the ex-husband to the late Mrs. Gorman . . .

and a woman he mistakenly thought was his step-son's girl-friend, Cassandra Drake."

Gorman's eyes wavered . . . hesitated . . . and then lifted up and stared at Turner.

"That's right, my friend," Turner nodded, his blue-gray eyes watching the man sitting directly across from him in fierce amusement. "You heard it. You made a mistake. You thought you killed Cassandra in her own apartment, but you didn't. You killed her sister, Kelly. An easy mistake. Kelly and Cassandra look like twins almost. But you didn't know that because Mark never introduced his girlfriend to either you or his mother."

Concanon, his face turning red with anger, glared at Turner. He started to say something but paused when he watched Frank reach down and pick up the remaining intact baseball bat.

"I know what you're going to ask, counselor. What possible motive would your client have for killing so many people? The answer is as simple as it is so commonplace. Money. Nothing more and nothing less. Money."

"Proof, detective? Do you have even the slightest iota of evidence to back these allegations up?"

Frank began slapping the heavy bat against the open palm of his left hand. The crude but surreal sound of his flesh and bone hitting the wooden bat resonated through the room. Even the doctor's eyes rotated back and looked at the scowling Frank for a moment.

"We have the testimony of Cassandra. She's claiming her boyfriend told her he was convinced his step-father was bilking every dime and nickel out of his mother's inheritance. We have phone records of John Wilson calling his son's cellphone repeatedly from the moment he got out of prison until his disappearance. Mark's father apparently had heard of the doctor's reputation as a liar and a blackmailer as it was well known among the prison inmates.

We have witnesses who will claim in court that Mark Wilson had made repeated inquiries to a number of university officials asking about his step-father's collegiate credentials. There was a question about their validity. Our inquiries came up with the interesting fact that no one remembered a Frank Gorman ever attending the university at all, much less achieving his numerous degrees.

And finally, counselor, there's this. We cannot find Mark Wilson. Nor his father. They have simply disappeared off the face of the earth. Odd, don't you think, that a son who was afraid his mother was being used and abused by his step-father would just simply . . . and mysteriously . . . disappear?"

"Circumstantial. Almost all of this evidence is either hearsay or circumstantial. I'll—"

CRACK!

Frank snapped the second back in half as if it were nothing more than a used toothpick. But the reaction was different. This time Frank Gorman flinched. Flinched as if he had been slapped in the face.

In the end the court agreed with us.

And Frank?

Frank handed over the five dollars and didn't say a word. Not one word.

9

PROOF

"Look, I'm telling you exactly what I think. Your boy is guilty. Guilty as sin and he's going to the electric chair for it. Once I present the prosecution's case against him he's as good as convicted. So get over it, you two. It's over. Open and shut."

And with those words, Assistant District Attorney Victor Koffsky turned, walked into a waiting elevator filled with irritable looking court house denizens of the bureaucracy, and disappeared from view, leaving us standing in the middle of the busy hallway with hands in our pockets and sour looks on our faces.

He was tall. Well dressed. Looked like an aging athlete who still kept himself in shape. Photogenic. With a perfect set of teeth as white as fine porcelain when he smiled.

I couldn't stand the sycophantic little asshole.

"Told'ya," Frank—my partner in Homicide—growled irritatingly. "I told you he wasn't going to listen. He's a frackin' gunslinger. All he wants to do is rack up another notch on his conviction's record. The 'sumbitch is going to run for the DA's office in a couple of years. He needs a glittering conviction record to be a viable candidate."

People, lots of people, were moving around us in the main hall in front of the bank of elevators of City Hall. Lawyers, cops, stenographers, reporters; the full gamut of what you would see on a busy Thursday afternoon. They were moving around us like rats scurrying through a maze. Most of them look constipated. Or worried. Or angry. All of them were too busy to care about why two big boned, ugly looking homicide detectives like us were standing in the middle of the hall looking like we had eaten a pot full of bad chili. Or worse.

"He's innocent, Frank. He's innocent. You know it and I know it. And to be honest, I think our assistant DA suspects it."

"Agreed," my mountain gorilla look alike nodded, glancing at the elevator. "But proof, boyo. We need proof. So I guess we'll have to play detectives and go out and find some."

A smirk played across my lips as I glanced at my partner. The red-haired, beady eyed giant of a man was almost telepathic. He knew we were going to do just exactly that.

"Come on, let's get out of here. It's too much of a madman's circus for my tastes. And I hate clowns."

The situation was like this. A patrol officer we knew named Jason Norris was found in bed with a dead woman. Dead because someone caved her head in with a ball peen hammer. The evidence pointed to Jason as the murderer. And I have to admit the evidence was compelling. The hammer's wooden handle was littered with Jason's finger prints. When they pulled Jason out of bed and arrested him, the victim's blood was smeared all over his hands. Semen—his—was you know where. Worse yet, the woman lying dead in bed beside him was six weeks pregnant.

Adding to Jason's woes—the content of alcohol in Jason's blood was enough to knock out an elephant.

That was the kicker. The alcohol content.

Jason had a reputation. A bad one. Everyone who knew him was aware of it. Since he was a cop it meant everyone in the department knew it. When Jason drank he couldn't stop. And when he got drunk he got mean. Really mean. But the worst part about his drinking was that he couldn't remember anything when he sobered up. Totally blacked out when he was drunk. There had been some bad times for Jason when he was drinking. Bar fights. The kind that led to back alley confrontations and beating the bejesus out of victims to the point where long hospital stays were necessary. Fights with his wife—fights that came to blows. Fights which led to his wife getting battered and bruised severely. Violence that would explode and become vicious.

It was his drinking and his tendency to get mean that caused his divorce. His wife and his children left him and had a court order put on him to keep him away from them forever. Three kids never to be seen again. A wife who once loved him now terrified of him and who had threatened to kill him if he ever showed up at her house.

His drinking got him suspended from the force. The second time, his shift commander told him the harsh truth. One more drunken binge and he was finished as a cop. Done for.

But, when sober, Jason Norris was the nicest guy you ever met. And one damn fine cop. You couldn't meet a better man. Honest, always laughing. Never getting riled up in those little situations cops who work the patrol beat get into on a weekly basis.

Steady as a rock and just as reliable. When sober. He worked in the patrol division down at South Side. Our precinct house. Frank and I were in the detective division. We saw Jason every day and chewed the fat with him. We'd seen him many times on various homicide cases we worked. We considered him a friend. A good friend.

So, when he asked us to come down and see him in the clinker and he told us—swore to us—that he did not kill his girl-friend nor had taken a drop of alcohol prior to having sex with her—we believed him.

Yeah. Two cynical, suspicious, garrulous, old veterans like us. We believed him.

We've seen it all. Heard it all.

The lies. The alibis.

The excuses.

Bad guys who thought they could get away with it. Basically good people who, for some reason or another, just cracked —just went over to the dark side—and killed someone. Greedy people who killed for personal gain. People acting stupid and winding up offing someone accidentally. We've seen it all. And all of them—all of them—would tell us in the beginning they were innocent. Misunderstood. Wrongly accused. Or it was an accident.

Heard it all.

Yeah. Sure, kid. Sure, you're innocent . . .

But when Jason told us, while he stood gripping the iron bars of his cell with white knuckles with a look of a deer caught in headlights, we believed him. We had no reason to believe him. We knew, the two of us, from experience that alcoholics regularly fell off the wagon and slinked back to the bottle. But not this time. This time we took a chance. Took a chance on an alcoholic's word. We believed him.

Walking out into the parking lot and moving toward my car, I slipped a pair of dark sunglasses on and looked at my red-haired gorilla of a partner. It was a hot August day. Hotter than Lucifer's day room. Hotter than an iron work's smelting pot. Walking across the scorching surface of an asphalt parking lot, past cars and pickup trucks that reflected sunlight into our faces, made it feel even hotter.

I was looking at Frank as we walked because I knew he was going to ask questions. As big and as ugly as the carrot-headed freak is, the guy is as smart as Einstein squared. I knew his micro-chipped computer for a mind was already looking over this case from about six different directions.

"The way I see it," he began as my red and white Rousch Ford Mustang came into view, "is we start on the idea that someone wants Jason behind bars. He's been framed by someone whose got a grudge."

I pulled out a set of car keys, unlocked my door, and opened it. Hitting the door lock button, I stood up and looked across the roof of the muscle car at Frank and grinned.

"Say that doesn't pan out. Say it's not someone holding a grudge against Jason. What's our other alternative?"

The rectangular shaped head of Frank's was about a foot and a half above the roofline of the Mustang as his beady little brown eyes bored into mine. There was a frown on his lips, and he was squinting at me with one eye. Like Popeye. Like he did every time there was a bright sun out.

"What are you not telling me, pretty boy? Come on, spit it out."

The grin on my lips widened as I slid into the hot interior of the car and closed the door. Frank slid into his as I started the 700-plus horse V8 engine and punched the air conditioner on. Frank looked like a surrealist painter's idea of a rejuvenated Neanderthal. Wide shoulders, rectangular head, arms as big as the anchor chains on the aircraft carrier Ronald Reagan. Tall. I was as tall as Frank. But I looked somewhat like a long dead actor. An actor from out of the '30's. Black hair, dark eyes, a thin mustache, an ever present smirk on my lips. Maybe a personality that went with the smirk. Or so I'm told.

Anyway. I was the pretty boy. He was the Neanderthal.

"A couple of months back, we were sitting in a booth at Dewey's drinking coffee. You were in the head using the bathroom. We were talking about families, married life—you know, just talking. Jason said he missed seeing his kids. I asked him if he thought he'd ever get married again and have another family. He looked up from his coffee cup and shook his head no. Told me he was going to get fixed. Make damn sure there'd be no way he'd get anyone pregnant again."

Dewey's was a diner down in the industrial section of town by the Brown River we liked to go to often. So did a lot of other cops. Like Jason.

"So you're thinking this isn't really about Jason. It's about the dead girl. And Jason's being used as a patsy," Frank growled, frowning, and looking at me.

"Could be," I nodded, depressing the clutch pedal and slapping the gearshift down into second gear to move. "If he got fixed. If the kid is not his."

"I know how to find out about the fixing part," Frank growled, reaching for his cellphone and bringing it up to his ear.

Two phone calls. One to the sergeant on the desk in the jail asking him to ask Jason the name of his personal doctor. The second call to the doctor. End results—Jason had been fixed. But there was a problem. Jason got himself fixed. But recently. Within the last three weeks. The embryo in the dead girl was at least six weeks old.

"So the baby could be his," I said as we drove in late afternoon traffic heading nowhere. "Did they do a DNA check on the baby to see if it was his?"

Another phone call. This time to the morgue. And the answer—not so good.

"No. They did not check the baby's DNA," Frank said,

snapping the phone closed and looking at me. "They didn't because that test is expensive, and they didn't think it was necessary. They could run one if you gave them the okay. But a DNA test takes weeks to get the results back."

Turning right onto a lesser traveled street, I accelerated and listened to the 700 plus horses of the engine in front of us rumbling pleasingly. Driving for a while, I confess, my mind was elsewhere. Thinking. Looking the case over. Until Frank's deep voice broke in.

"Still think our boy is innocent?"

"Still think so," I nodded, frowning. "Everything the DA has on Jason could have been planted as much as being the real deal."

"But the blood alcohol level. How'd he get drunk if he didn't do any drinking?"

I frowned again and shook my head. The car moved like a killer whale skimming the ocean surf looking for seals to munch on. I was driving away from the downtown traffic bog but with no particular place in mind, something we did often when we were working a case and found ourselves in the batter's box called indecision.

"Call forensics again and ask Joe to read us the toxicology report."

Joe was Joe Weiser. Lab tech and forensics expert. A gum smacking, constant smirking, pimple-faced, whiz kid who was good at his job. And someone we trusted.

Frank was on the phone for five minutes while I was driving. When he hung up, there was a twitch in the man's lips —the closest Frank came to grinning.

"Amphetamines. Enough to knock out Jason and keep him down for hours. And get this—Joe said Jason had a needle mark between the big toe and middle toe of his right foot. Big bruise. The works."

I nodded and glanced at Frank.

Someone could knock out his victim with amphetamines and slowly feed him an IV of alcohol. Just enough alcohol to make a breath-analyzer go berserk.

"Time to start looking at the victim I'd say."

"Me too," Frank agreed.

Cop work.

Three-quarters of the routine was day-to-day questioning. One-quarter intuition. You ask questions. The same questions mostly, over and over again. You watch the faces of those you talk to. Watch their eyes. Watch their hands. Watch how they sit in a chair. Listen to the timbre of their voices. The little things. Always the little things.

It's not so much what they say. It's how they say it. And what they say to you without saying a word. Sometimes witnesses and suspects tell a cop more that way than what they reveal from their statements.

A good example of this would be Doctor Thomas Pope.

Pope kept folding his hands on his lap as he sat in a chair in his office and talked to us. Dr. Pope was a gynecologist. The dead woman, by the way, was Holly Harris. Nurse Holly Harris happened to be the main nurse in Dr. Pope's private practice.

Late that afternoon, Frank and I came calling on Dr. Pope at his office. It was the end of the day, and the good doctor was about to leave and go home for the night—home to his lovely wife, his five bedroom house, his evening with the wife at the club having some drinks and sharing a meal with friends.

"Just a couple of questions, doctor. Just a couple of minutes of your time. That's all we're asking," I said as we stood facing each other.

"Well," the deep voice of the man said as he hurriedly looked at the thousand dollar Rolex strapped to his wrist and then up at us. "Okay. But I haven't much time. I'm to pick the wife up at six and then we have a dinner at the club with the mayor and a few other friends."

Thomas Pope was in his early fifties. Salt and pepper colored hair. Blue eyes. Good teeth. A deep, natural tan. Good looking. Neither thin nor fat. He wore an Armani suit with a red silk tie around his neck, with a big diamond pin stuck smack in the middle.

"I don't really understand why I am talking to two different detectives, gentlemen. I though this case was closed, and the guilty party was behind bars."

"That's why we're here," Frank said, eyeing the elaborate office complex of the doctor's as we walked back to his office. "A question has arisen about the evidence."

"Oh?" Pope said, looking up at us after sitting down on a black, leather divan in his office, crossing his legs, and folding his hands onto his lap. "What's been discovered, if I may ask?"

"Actually, a couple of new discoveries," I said after we sat down on a divan directly opposite the doctor. "A couple of points that throw a different light on the case."

Hands.

Refolding themselves. Or reaching out and adjusting the angle of a magazine lying on the coffee table between us before refolding again.

"Oh?"

"We just found out the police officer charged with murder has a big bruise on his foot. Between a couple of toes, apparently put there by someone using a syringe. Amphetamines were found in his blood, as well as alcohol. A really large amount of amphetamines."

"Sounds like the man was a drug user as well as an alcoholic," the doctor said, smiling sadly.

Hands.

Moving. Unable to keep still.

I smiled.

"The police officer has a past with alcoholism, that's true. But not drugs. He's never been known to use drugs. So it's something new for us to look at."

"I'm afraid, from my experience in dealing with my patients, sooner or later an alcoholic gets involved with drugs. I understand this man was rather violent when he drank. Hollie mentioned to me a couple of times her concerns for her safety when he became inebriated."

"She said her boyfriend was hitting the booze some?" Frank asked, as he tried not to watch the doctor's hands.

"I'm afraid so, detective. Apparently he liked his whiskey. And lots of it."

Hands. Moving. This time to straighten his tie underneath his suit coat before folding them onto his lap.

"Yes, his blood alcohol count was quite high," I agreed and smiled. "But being a doctor and all, maybe you could make a comment on a theory of ours. You know, tell us if it's feasible to fake the results. Make it look like a man's drunk even though he hasn't drunk a drop."

Hands. Hands rubbing each other gently.

"What's your theory?"

"We've been talking. Trying to come up with a possible defense for the accused. An expert like you might be able to say if it's possible or not for it to be done," I said, looking straight into the doctor's blue eyes.

"Yes?"

"Slip a Mickey into the guy's coffee or tea," Frank said, his eyes unblinking as he stared at the doctor. "You know, a knock out potion. A Mickey. Big enough to knock the guy out. And knocked out, you take a needle attached to an intra-venous feeding system and stuff enough alcohol in him to make him drunk. Is it possible for something like that to happen?"

This time not the hands. The eyes.

The eyes widening. Ever so slightly. The look of panic for a heartbeat or two. And then back to normal.

"Well . . . I suppose that could be done. Yes, technically possible. But it sounds a bit farfetched, don't you think? Especially with the man's reputation? Why would anyone what to be so . . . so ingenious coming up with a plan like that?"

"Ah, that brings us to the second piece of evidence," I said, the smile on my lips widening. "It seems like the victim was six weeks pregnant. I'm thinking she didn't know. The accused didn't know. In fact the accused couldn't have impregnated her since he had himself surgically altered to keep that from happening. So whoever killed our victim, already knew she was pregnant before the mother even knew. Motive enough, I suspect, for someone to develop a plan."

Hands.

Coming up to his lips and swiping downward. His eyes filled with horror. Guilty. As guilty as sin and knowing we knew it. We knew it and waited for him to say something. Say something to possibly defend himself. But he saw it in our faces. We had proof. There was the six week old fetus. DNA. His DNA.

Hands. Folding.

Laying on his lap.

For the last time.

"She didn't know she was pregnant. Of course I knew. The other night she came into the office and said we were through. Done. No more sex. I could keep my wife and my golf club privileges. She said she found someone and had fallen in love. She was quitting. Leaving me. We were through. I . . . I went crazy. I kept wondering to myself, could I trust her? Would she keep her promise and never reveal the true identity of her child's father?

I never considered myself a vindictive, possessive kind of man. But I couldn't take it. Couldn't take the thought of losing her. Every time I touched her my whole body exploded with a desire to possess her. I . . . I couldn't let go! I couldn't bear the thought of losing her. Especially losing her to an alcohol has-been of a cop."

Later that night we roused Assistant District Attorney Victor Koffsky out of his bed. We pounded. Rudely on the front door, leaned on the doorbell, and shouted, waking up the neighbors in the posh suburban neighborhood of his, until he came to the door. When he threw the door open he was pissed. Pissed enough to chew nails. Too bad. We told him to get his ass into some clothes and come downtown with us. It was time to let an innocent man out of jail. He didn't argue. He saw it in our eyes. We meant it.

He came quietly.

10

DIRT

H e was scared.
　　　　Nervous.
Suspicious.

As we sat in the booth watching him through the big plate glass window of Dewey's, we could tell he was wound up tighter than a cheap wristwatch. His head kept darting back and forth with quick, jerking movements. Several times he stopped, turned, and scanned the streets behind him. He paused often . . . nervously hesitating before crossing streets. Hesitating as if he was expecting a cement truck to come along and turn him into a grease stain at any moment.

Cupping his hands in front of his face, he blew some warmth in them before stuffing them into his dark blue seaman's coat. Down by the river it was colder than a Siberian nightmare—as it always was in late January in this city. Wearing a blue stocking sock hat pulled down over his ears, hot puffs of steam shot from his mouth in rapid machine gun bursts as the little man paused and studied the parking lot of the diner in front of him.

Yeah. It didn't take much to see Davie Higgins was one frightened little thief.

Darting across the street, zig zagging like a star NFL running back in a Sunday afternoon game, Davie made his way through traffic and navigated the parking lot of the diner. He came through the door and into the warmth of the diner in one fast, smooth motion—his eyes taking in everyone with a quick, practiced glance. When he saw us in our usual place, he moved rapidly to join us.

I slid over in the booth to make room for him and nodded to Dewey to bring over a cup of hot, coal black java. Davie would need a lot of java to thaw out on a day like today. And Dewey, the owner of this joint, made coffee strong enough to shut down a runaway nuclear reactor.

Dewey's is one of our favorite eateries. It's a big aluminum eatery straight out of the 50's sitting down by the river. Good food. Easy on the wallet. Frank—my partner in Homicide for the last five years—and I ate there often. As do a number of other cops working with us out of the South Side precinct.

"Guys, tha . . . .thanks for meeting me here like this."

Frank, the red-bearded gorilla that was my partner, nodded and pointed to the coffee cup sliding across the table.

"Thaw out first, and then talk. I'm getting cold just looking at'ya."

A grin flashed across Davie's haggard, unshaven face as he reached for the coffee with both hands. You could almost see the coffee thawing his frozen flesh.

We let him drink the first cup of java and then waited for Dewey to refill it before we spoke.

"Okay, Danny. What's up? Your call sounded urgent."

He lowered the cup, still gripping it with both hands, and shot glances at the two of us and then at the few still sitting in the diner. You could see it in his face and eyes—he wanted to talk. You could also catch a glimpse of genuine fear holding him back.

"Listen, guys, I've got to get out of town. I've got to leave now. Even sitting here talking to you two is costing me. But the thing is . . . I need some dough. So I thought of you, Turn. I hear you're loaded. Thought maybe you could loan me a few bucks."

I looked into the little man's face, half expecting the thief to break into a big grin. This sounded like a joke. One of Davie's famous practical jokes. He had pulled a few on me before. Even had Frank in on the joke. But the look in his eyes, of a deer running from the wolves, convinced me this wasn't a joke. This was real.

"What happened, Davie?" Frank grunted, reaching for his coffee and glancing out the big picture window beside him. Looking for something that might be out-of-place maybe. Like maybe a car with two men sitting in it with the car running— looking as if they were waiting for someone.

Davie leaned across the table half way and lowered his voice to barely above a whisper.

"I saw someone get snuffed last night. Saw it with my own eyes. Saw the two of'em grab this chick and throw a pillow over her face. She fought. She kicked. She tried to escape. But these guys were good. They knew what they were doing."

Frank shot me a glance and gave me a slight nod toward the window.

My eyes barely moved. But it was enough.

In the parking lot about six rows back, two guys in heavy trench coats sat in a black Caddy Seville. The driver had both hands on the wheel, and he was wearing black leather gloves. Both of them had fedoras on and pulled down low over the eyes. There was no way to catch a good glimpse of their faces.

The little thief didn't see the car. He was too busy slurping hot coffee and digging into a big donut Dewey brought over and shoved in front of him on the table.

"Start from the beginning," I said, keeping my eyes on the little man and not looking anywhere else. "Tell us everything."

"Yeah, yeah . . . I know the routine. I was . . well . . . working a heist last night. Over on Belmont drive. You know. That little art museum some rich widow built a few years ago. That place."

I nodded. I knew exactly where he was last night. I knew exactly what he was doing. Coming on duty tonight one of the daily bulletins was a report about a very expensive piece of canvas lifted out of the Harlin Museum over on Belmont.

"Go on," I said, reaching for my donut.

"I was using a rope and lowering myself down from a skylight, see. 'Bout half way down I glance up and out of one of their tall windows. Across the street from the museum is a fancy apartment complex. The rear of a fancy complex. All the balconies face the museum. Well, I see this blond chick stagger into sight. She's left the curtains to the glass balcony door wide open, and I could see her as clear as day. About twenty-five . . . maybe thirty. Tops."

Frank was listening and taking in every word. But his eyes were on the two men in the car. Apparently the two in the car noticed Frank's interest. From out of the side of my eye, I saw a dark shape slide out of the Dewey's lot and disappear.

"I could see she's agitated. Scared. She pressed her back up against the glass and throws a hand out as if to push someone away. That's when . . . that's when the two big men grabbed her and strangled her with the pillow."

"Describe 'em," Frank grunted, turning his attention toward the little man in front of him.

"I didn't catch a glimpse of their faces that time, Frank. Like I said, the girl put up a fight. They were twisting and turning around like crazy yo-yo's for a while until one of 'em got a hold of her from behind and held her still."

"So you didn't see their faces," I repeated.

"Not that time, Turn. Not that time. But a couple of minutes later I saw a face. After the chick slumped over they dragged her back into apartment. But one of'em came back and closed the curtains."

"Recognize him?" Frank grunted, glancing out the big plate glass window again.

Davie didn't immediately answer. The little guy shuddered violently. The color in his face drained. He became as pale as one of the corpses lying in the city morgue. His eyes looked like a trapped animal as his hands lifted the cup of java to his lips and took a long drag of the scalding black joe.

"I . . . I think he saw me, guys. Saw me somehow hanging on the rope in the museum. That's the reason I gotta get out town. If he did see me I'm as good as dead. That sonofabitch doesn't play around. He'll cut my throat in the blink of an eye. You've got to believe me, guys! I can't stay here! I gotta leave . . . get the hell out of here and go as far away from here as I can possibly get!"

"Who saw you?" I asked quietly. "Give us a name and we'll go over and pinch'em. We'll make sure they won't come after you."

"Ha!" A sardonic bark for a laugh escaped from the little man's lips as he lowered his coffee cup and shook his head in amused helplessness. "You're not going to pinch these guys. I've never heard of a cop pinching a cop. Besides, even if you did, where would it get you? I'm leaving town, boys. I'm not sticking around—and sure as hell I ain't gonna testify again- st'em. I may look stupid, but I ain't that stupid."

"You're saying a cop killed this woman?"

"I saw Mickey Mulligan's ugly grinning face just as clearly

as I'm seeing yours, Frank. The asshole came to the window, chewing that damn toothpick he's always chewing on, looked out to see if anyone was curious, and then closed the curtains. Plain as day."

Mickey Mulligan was detective sergeant Mickey Mulligan. A detective, Homicide section, based out of the Downtown division of the city's police force. His partner was named Iggie Johansson.

Cops.

Dirty. Dirty but smart. A lot in the department believed the two were on the take. Worked as the muscle for a local crime boss. Both Frank and I knew them quite well. We had had our share of run-ins with them.

It would have given us great pleasure to be able to cuff them and bring them in on some kind of provable rap. Like maybe—homicide.

"And you think he saw you," I said, frowning. "Saw you through a window inside the museum in the dead of night?"

"Maybe he did—maybe he didn't. Hell, I'm too damn scared to know for sure. All I know is this. If he thinks someone saw him standing in that window right after killing that girl, they're as good as dead. And I'm not sticking around to find out what happens next. So I'm asking, Turner . . . asking as a guy whose given the two of you a lot of good tips on other shit going down in this town . . . I'm asking if you'll spot me some money."

I frowned and glanced at my watch. It was almost four in the afternoon. The nearest branch of my bank was ten blocks away. It'd take, in this afternoon traffic, a good hour to get there and get back. An hour I didn't want Davie to endure alone.

"Let's go," I said, half pushing the little thief out of the booth.

"Where we going?" he asked, sliding out and turning to stare at me.

"Nearest ATM is about five blocks from here. I can pull out maybe five C-notes. I can get you more tomorrow if you're willing to stick around."

"Not me, brother," Dave said, shaking his head, his voice sounded firm. "Five hundred is more than enough. I know where I'm going and that'll be enough to get me there."

"We'd feel a lot better if you'd let us tuck you away some place nice and safe for a while. Just for the night. You know, just in case, and then in the morning we'll see you off," Frank growled but spoke softly.

"Thanks, guys. For everything. But I know how to take care of myself. Where I'm going no one is going to find me."

And with those last words he left us in front of the ATM. Left us in the cold. Walked away, hailed for a cab, and disappeared into the heavy traffic. We watched the cab leave, each of us in our silence, knowing the dumb sonofabitch wasn't going to make it through the night alive.

We drove over to The Esquires, the apartment complex Davie said he had seen a murder committed. It didn't take long to find the body. She was swinging from a sheet tied around a wooden ceiling beam. Below her dangling feet was a chair that had been kicked away. On a glass coffee table was a typed-written suicide letter. A typed letter with no signature.

"Davie's in a world of shit if this is really a murder," Frank growled, frowning and shaking his head. "If Mulligan saw him hanging by a rope in the museum, our little friend hasn't got a snowball's chance in hell."

I nodded, turned, and walked to the drapes that hid the sliding glass door that led out onto the balcony. Pulling them open, I gazed out across the street and into the glass window of the museum where Davie said he was when he saw Mickey Mulligan. It was roughly the same time of night as it was when the murder went down. Not to my surprise I noticed there was enough back light in the museum to see fairly clearly inside. Maybe not enough light to see a face. But more than enough light to see a dark form hanging from a rope in midair.

Iggie and Mickey were smart enough to figure it out. It wouldn't take long to figure out that the only second-story man with the experience, and confidence, to rob a high security museum was Davie.

I reached for the cellphone inside my coat and called for Joe Weiser and his forensics team. I then dialed our shift commander Lt. Yankovich and told him we had to sit down and talk. Two hours later, we were sitting in the lieutenant's office with the door closed and watching him use a long boney finger to rub the throbbing vein pulsating visibly in his forehead.

"Those fuckers," he grunted, shaking his head and sounding savage. "They've been playing both sides of the fence for years. I've been waiting to collar them and bring them in since the first day I met them. But they're good. They're experts in covering their tracks. Betcha fifty the coroner is going to come up with a report that is, at best, inconclusive. She could have been murdered by strangulation. But the hanging covered up all traces."

That's what we were thinking. It wasn't as if we had not had our run-ins with Iggie and Mickey before. A year prior the two had snuffed out a couple of friends of ours but made it appear as if it was a murder-suicide.

"The pissy thing is I can't say a damn thing to the chief of detectives about this. Nor can I mention it to internal affairs. The chief thinks these two bastards are top notch detectives. They're a couple of his boys. And internal affairs doesn't want to hear anything without some tangible evidence to back up the claims. In other words, boys, without some evidence that will implicate them in this murder, we've got nothing. Too bad your little thief wouldn't hang around and talk. But I understand his reasons why he'd think otherwise."

"We'll find some evidence, Yank. If the lab comes back and can't give us a definitive decision and say it's a murder, what we need from you is to label it as a Suspicious Fatality."

"Ah. . . I see where this is going," the lieutenant nodded, smiling. "You think the two believe they got away clean with this murder. But a Suspicious Fatality makes it an official inquiry. You want to draw them into this mess. Make them fidgety. There's no love lost between you and them. You think they may do something stupid and tip their hand. Good. I like it."

As we walked out of the lieutenant's office, Frank pulled out his cellphone and began punching in numbers.

"Home?" I asked.

"Naw," he said, shaking his massive head. "If Iggie and Mickey were in on this then this girl is somehow connected to their boss."

Nathan Brinkley.

A lot of people thought the smooth, well-dressed, handsome, professional gambler ran the town. I wouldn't offer up too much of an argument against the idea. Brinkley's sticky fingers seemed to be everywhere in city politics. He was especially strong in ward politics down at the grassroots level. He had a knack for glad-handing people and making them feel important—while he ran a shiv through their heart in the process.

But so far the man had been meticulous in keeping his name out of the papers and totally removed from any criminal accusation. The press loved the guy. It seemed he was on the local news every night of the week.

A few phone calls—some promises given we could keep to a few associates—and we got what we were looking for. The dead girl used to be Nathan Brinkley's main squeeze. She was a high-priced model he met in New York. Great looks. Great listener. Talked a lot when she got drunk. Couldn't keep her mouth shut. Apparently said a couple of things at some local nightclubs that really upset Brinkley.

"She became a liability," Frank nodded, snapping his phone closed after his last phone call. "Knew too much and couldn't keep her mouth shut."

"So Brinkley tells Iggie and Mickey to clean up the mess. Do it quietly and efficiently."

I started to say something, but my cellphone started buzzing.

"Turner, listen. . . there's a contract out on me. Two hired guns from Detroit flew in last night to take me out. Word is a certain person we know thinks I know too much. They've got this town buttoned up. I can't move anywhere without being seen. I. . . I need your help."

It was Davie talking. And he sounded—odd.

"Davie, where are you? Let us come and get you and take you someplace safe."

"Yeah . . . yeah, that makes sense. There's eyes everywhere looking for me. I'm over at my girl's apartment. Corner of Douglas and Haig, apartment 22."

"Davie, lock the doors and keep away from the windows. We'll be over there in ten minutes."

Took us eighteen minutes to get to Douglas and Haig. Rolling out of the car we both looked the place over and frowned. It was an old hotel down in the bad end of town. A dive where those who worked the streets at night, or ran numbers for the big boys, could afford to live in. The moment our eyes took it in we had bad vibrations.

"You thinking what I'm thinking?" the ugly mug of a partner asked me as he unbuttoned his sport jacket casually.

"If you're thinking the last scene of Butch Cassidy and the Sundance Kid then yeah, that's what I'm thinking."

A trap. It felt like a trap. It looked like the perfect place for a trap. It smelled like a trap. Unbuttoning my coat, I reached in and pulled out the heavy framed .45 cal. Kimber and slid the carriage back to jack a round into the firing chamber. From behind my back, I reached for the .380 cal. Walther PPK I used as a back-up gun.

We went in quietly. Entering the front door, we found ourselves in a long corridor filled with the smells of a hundred different varieties. On either side of the corridor was a long stretch of apartment doors—all closed and conspicuously silent. To our left, a set of creaky, ancient-looking stairs that went up to the second floor. As quietly as we could, we went up the stairs, guns drawn and anticipating the fireworks to begin at any moment.

We found the door to apartment 22 partially open. Frank, using the muzzle of his 9 mil. Glock, pushed the door open further while I stood in the hall, my back to him, waiting for someone to step out from one of the apartments with a gun in his hand.

"Davie's dead," Frank growled behind me. "Just happened. He's still bleeding, and can you smell the cordite?"

A door flew open. And then a second door. Two guys stepped out into the hall with Uzi's in their hands. The hallway erupted in gunfire. I dove for the floor, firing both guns at one of the shooters in the process. Frank knelt down and started firing at the other target. The hail of machine gun fire was incredibly loud and incredibly destructive. Bullets spraying from the stubby muzzles of each Uzi chewed up the walls, throwing clouds of flying splinters everywhere. From within one of the apartments a woman started screaming hysterically.

And then it was over as fast as it started. Our two shooters ducked back into their respective rooms and disappeared completely. The surprised look I aimed toward my partner was obvious. But more surprises awaited us. Coming to my feet, I heard another set of doors open behind me with a loud bang. Turning, lifting the Kimber up rapidly, I saw two more shooters emerge into the hall. This time they had shotguns, the ugly muzzles up, and already pointing at us. But before I had time to move—before Frank had time to turn—gunfire erupted and I saw the two shooters stagger back from being hit by multiple rounds.

Surprised at this unexpected rescue, I turned to see who our saviors were.

Iggie Johansson and Mickey Mulligan.

Both of them, standing at the top of the stairs with guns in their hands, stood looking at us with smirks on their faces. And behind them? Two newspaper reporters and two photographers. Reporters from a paper owned by Nathan Brinkley. The photographers were clicking shots as fast as their fingers could work their cameras. The two reporters came rushing from behind Iggie and Mickey and ran toward us with digital recorders lifted up to catch every word we said.

How does it feel to be rescued by detectives Johansson and Mulligan? Care to comment on how we knew Davie Higgins was involved in the murder of a beautiful model? Who sent out these hired guns to kill you? Do you believe your two friends should be given a medal for saving your lives?

I turned and looked at the smirking face of Iggie Johansson. The dark complexioned, dark eyed man with the toothpick between his lips, stared back. The smirk on his lips widened as he lifted a hand up and half saluted me.

There would be no catching Iggie and Mickey and charging them with murder. By nightfall, the papers of Nathan Brinkley would have the story out in blazing color on their front pages hailing these two as heroes. The chief of detectives would be quoted often about how highly he thought of these two detectives and the work that they did. They would get their medals for valor, penned on their chests by the mayor himself.

And Nathan Brinkley? Nathan Brinkley would be laughing. Laughing in a pleased Cheshire-cat smugness at again thwarting our efforts to bring him down.

Dear reader,

We hope you enjoyed reading *Guns, Gams, Ghosts and Gangsters*. Please take a moment to leave a review, even if it's a short one. Your opinion is important to us.

Discover more books by B.R. Stateham at https://www.nextchapter.pub/authors/br-stateham

Want to know when one of our books is free or discounted? Join the newsletter at http://eepurl.com/bqqB3H

Best regards,

B.R. Stateham and the Next Chapter Team

You might also like:
Evil Arises by B.R. Stateham

To read the first chapter for free, please head to:
https://www.nextchapter.pub/books/evil-arises

ABOUT THE AUTHOR

B.R. Stateham is a seventy-two year old curmudgeon with an unhinged imagination that never stops thinking up new stories. Like the Turner Hahn/Frank Morales tales. There are, currently, four novels and two collections of short-stories featuring these two. With more to come.

But the author has other characters out there. Living and working in their own respective worlds. Worlds of dark noir to worlds of off-world fantasies. Again—with more to come.

Guns, Gams, Ghosts and Gangsters
ISBN: 978-4-86751-674-4

Published by
Next Chapter
1-60-20 Minami-Otsuka
170-0005 Toshima-Ku, Tokyo
+818035793528

6th July 2021

CPSIA information can be obtained
at www.ICGtesting.com
Printed in the USA
BVHW032058260721
612869BV00001B/59

9 784867 516744